Just Sheaffer

IAN MOWATT

Just Sheaffer

HUTCHINSON OF LONDON

HUTCHINSON & CO (*Publishers*) LTD
3 Fitzroy Square, London W1

London Melbourne Sydney Auckland
Wellington Johannesburg Cape Town
and agencies throughout the world

First published in Great Britain 1974

© Ian Mowatt 1973

*This book has been set in Plantin type, printed in Great Britain
on antique wove paper by Anchor Press, and
bound by Wm. Brendon, both of Tiptree, Essex*

ISBN 0 09 118400 2

For Hiram Haydn

*and with special thanks
to
David Campbell
Lizzie and Dave*

Saturday

I

SHEAFFER belched, spluttered, belched again. Then he thought of a few disgusting words, said them aloud, and felt very much better. Still, he thought, what a bloody day; first the all-night drive from London, only four hours' sleep, and now registration; tedious, boring, monotonous; really awful, in fact. He scooped two teaspoonfuls of dehydrated milk into his coffee and watched it sink and rise in the green plastic cup; then stirred it cautiously to avoid lumps. Clusters of congealed particles drifted unappetisingly to the surface and whirled around in the circular path of the spoon. He tasted it; too hot; a bit soapy. Sheaffer sighed and reached for the radio; he dressed and shaved to the one o'clock news.

The corridor of floor 12 was hot and the air was muggy. Someone had smashed the light of the lift button with a sharp instrument; or perhaps, thought Sheaffer, it was with a blunt one, the kind they use in murders. He stood in a daze for a moment or so with the expression of one about to be committed. At last the lift arrived.

Drrring.

Going down, said the arrows.

Sheaffer walked in and nodded to a young woman in the left-hand corner; the doors closed. He watched the numbers above the door with early-morning interest.

11 . . . 10 . . . 9 . . . Keep going . . . good . . . keep it up . . . easy now . . . Bet it stops at 7 . . . No. Sure to stop at 2 though. . . .

He looked across at the young woman and smiled. . . . Married probably . . . yes, definitely . . . homely, stable look about her . . .

'Wouldn't it be absolutely *dreadful*,' said the young woman suddenly, out of the blue, 'if it stuck between floors?'

Sheaffer thought for a bit and said, 'Sure.'

The lift stopped at floor 5 and a painter who looked like Ernest Hemingway came in, dressed in white overalls and carrying a paint roller in one hand. Hemingway, thought Sheaffer. . . . Hemingway . . . Ernest himself . . . no . . . can't be . . . dead . . . definitely dead . . . killed himself . . . could be his brother . . . reborn perhaps . . . fancy a bit of painting Ernest . . . can't ask him though . . . Excuse me, is your name Hemingway? . . . Drop dead. . . . Probably gets jokes about it all the time. . . .

Clunk.

The lift hit the ground floor with an unexpected jolt. The young woman shuddered; the paint roller fell on the carpeted floor.

'Shit,' said the man who looked like Ernest Hemingway; then picked up his roller and apologised to the young woman for saying, 'shit'.

The lift doors opened.

' 'Bye,' said Sheaffer. He walked into the street and sniffed fresh air; a leafy smell; tasty. A light breeze carried it effortlessly to his nostrils. Good to be back, he thought. He jumped into his car, started the engine. . . . First time . . . great . . . He pulled out from the kerb and headed for All Saints.

Father Scraw paused in the aisle of All Saints Episcopal Church and sniffed; sweet-smelling incense, stale from the morning's service; pleasing to the nostrils, he thought, and shuffled through to the back courtyard. Sheaffer walked slowly behind like a pallbearer, his vision obscured by the cases of best altar wine he was carrying. Father Scraw reached the storeroom and unlocked the door. Dust everywhere; on the floor, a box, half full of candles, and a badly tarnished chalice in a heap of straw. He breathed a mouthful of dust and coughed.

'Where shall I put them, Father?' asked Sheaffer a little impatiently; time was getting on; better leave at least an hour for registration.

Father Scraw pointed to the centre of the floor.

'Fine,' said Sheaffer. He gently lowered the two cases to the ground; they were made of cardboard, brown and unmarked; no writing; no advertisements; no firm; nothing even to tell you what it was, thought Sheaffer. . . . Rather like confidential pregnancy tests . . . You will receive a plain brown envelope. . . . Or when you order contraceptives by mail . . . or very dirty books . . .

Back outside the air tasted even better than before.

'You know, Sheaffer,' said Father Scraw meditatively, 'we can never thank you enough for your help.'

'Nonsense,' said Sheaffer. 'Any time—a great pleasure.'

'Well,' said Father Scraw, 'thank you anyway. How, by the way, is your father these days?'

'Well,' said Sheaffer, 'he's very healthy, except that his sleepwalking is getting worse. We've stopped him getting out of the house now, but he still wanders all over it—turns on the taps and things—a bit messy at times.'

'Yes,' sympathised Father Scraw, 'it must be. But otherwise he's fine, is he?'

'Well,' said Sheaffer gravely, 'actually, Father, he's thinking of becoming a Catholic.'

'A phase,' said Father Scraw, stroking his chin, 'through which many great men pass.'

'Well,' continued Sheaffer, 'he has this thing about damnation at the moment.' He paused. 'Something which, of course, has never bothered me, since I don't believe in Hell.'

'No,' said Father Scraw. 'Neither do I.'

'Anyway,' said Sheaffer, 'Mother says he prays aloud now on his knees, instead of silently in bed. But apparently he hasn't started praying for the souls of the dead yet.'

'Oh good,' said Father Scraw. 'Then there's still hope.'

'A little,' said Sheaffer, not sounding too hopeful. 'Anyway, Father, I'll let you know. I must go now—registration, you know.'

Father Scraw thanked him again.

'Remember to come round any time, Sheaffer.'

'Thanks,' said Sheaffer, 'I will.' He walked leisurely down the grass path, whistling the tune of 'Jesus wants me for a sunbeam' with exaggerated simplicity. Great guy, Scraw, he thought. . . . Really great . . . glad he doesn't believe in Hell . . . security in numbers . . . pity about Dad though . . . snap out of it maybe . . . hope so . . . must call tonight . . .

He reached the gate, turned and waved to Father Scraw, and walked around the corner to register.

Sheaffer ran up the steps of Henderson Hall and stopped at the reception desk. . . . No one . . . ridiculous . . . still eating probably . . . this is what we pay our fees for . . . absurd . . . Perhaps, he thought, mollifying, she was suddenly taken ill. . . . Rushed to hospital . . . burst appendix . . . sorry, Miss, nothing we can do . . . dead on arrival . . . funeral Saturday . . . no flowers, please . . . Then he saw a small silver bell and a notice that said RING FOR SERVICE. He took the bell in his hand, smiled, and rang it loudly three times. The door opened. A fat woman who looked about twenty-five waddled in and sat down at the desk. Pimples, thought Sheaffer. . . . Pimples . . . poor soul . . . should use Wendy with moisturising cream . . . for a cool, clear complexion . . .

'Yes?' said the young woman impatiently.

'I was wondering,' said Sheaffer, feeling important, 'where I should go to register.'

'Name?' said the woman.

'Sheaffer,' said Sheaffer.

'In that case,' said the woman, her face brightening, 'you should have registered yesterday.' She looked up at Sheaffer and smiled. 'You will, of course, be liable to a five-pound late fee.'

'Wonderful,' said Sheaffer, 'perfectly wonderful—but what do I do about it now?'

'Through the swing doors,' said the fat woman imperiously.

'Thank you,' said Sheaffer, 'very much indeed, for your invaluable assistance.'

Sheaffer strutted through the swing doors and into a vast hall brimful of desks and of students who sat scribbling on different-coloured pieces of paper. On the far wall there was a portrait of Henderson, after whom the hall had been named. Sheaffer discovered where desk S was and walked up to the old woman sitting at it. Knitting, he thought. . . . Knitting . . . damned all else to do anyway . . . only waiting for people like me . . . and their five pounds . . . vultures . . .

'Good morning,' said Sheaffer.

'Good afternoon,' said the old woman, 'I'm Mrs. Ellsmere. Can I help you?'

'Yes,' said Sheaffer. 'My name is Sheaffer and I would like to register.'

'Well, you've come to the right table,' said Mrs. Ellsmere.

'Yes,' said Sheaffer.

'It's amazing how many people don't,' said Mrs. Ellsmere. 'I've had C's and F's, and even one X wandered over.'

'Really,' said Sheaffer.

'You appreciate,' said Mrs. Ellsmere, sounding very sorry about it, 'that you're late.'

'Yes,' said Sheaffer. 'Five pounds, isn't it?' He took five pounds from his wallet and handed the note to the old woman.

'You realise,' said Mrs. Ellsmere, smiling, 'that you can pay it in instalments if you wish.'

'Oh no,' said Sheaffer, 'please no. I might not sleep at night if I thought I owed the University money.'

Mrs. Ellsmere smiled, accepted the five-pound note, and handed Sheaffer his registration forms. He took them and sat himself down at the nearest desk.

. . . Always fill in the easy ones first. . . . Name . . . home address . . . term address . . . good, that's them out of the way. . . . Now for the computerised form . . . God, they know my name . . . and date of birth . . . and subject. . . . Not this though . . . height in inches . . . funny . . . never think of it like that . . . five twelves are sixty and eight is sixty-eight . . . good . . . good . . . easier than I thought. . . . He raced through 'sex', 'country of origin', 'nationality', and 'telephone number', stopping abruptly at 'occupation of father' and 'religion'. He consulted his book of instructions.

Mrs. Ellsmere looked up from her knitting and smiled. 'Back again, Mr. Sheaffer?'

'Yes,' said Sheaffer. 'I have a problem. My father is not a fisherman.'

'Well,' said Mrs. Ellsmere, sympathetically, 'neither was mine.'

Sheaffer laid the computerised form on the table. 'You see,' he said, 'it's not quite as simple as that. Here the computer has written "Fisherman" opposite "Occupation of Father". Now, although it is true that my father has fished, he has never made a living from it, or indeed ever caught more than enough for one meal.'

'I see,' said Mrs. Ellsmere. 'There must be a mistake.' She erased 'Fisherman' with a special computer eraser. 'What does your father do, then, Mr. Sheaffer?'

'Nothing,' said Sheaffer.

'Nothing,' repeated Mrs. Ellsmere.

'Nothing at all,' said Sheaffer.

'Oh,' said Mrs. Ellsmere, smiling. 'He's retired then?'

'No,' said Sheaffer emphatically. 'He has nothing to re-tire from.'

'Unemployed, then?' asked Mrs. Ellsmere hopefully.

'No, not that either,' said Sheaffer. 'That suggests he would work if he could. But he's never wanted to.'

Mrs. Ellsmere sighed. 'Has he ever done anything at all?' she asked.

'Well,' said Sheaffer, 'I believe he was an underground publisher many years ago. Of course, that was before his first conversion.'

'Of course,' said Mrs. Ellsmere, wondering what was coming next. She puzzled for a moment. 'How about one-time publisher?' she suddenly suggested.

'That's better,' said Sheaffer, 'than fisherman. But couldn't we just leave it blank?'

'Oh *no*,' said Mrs. Ellsmere quickly. 'No one is allowed to leave *anything* blank.'

'Very well then,' said Sheaffer, reluctantly reconciled to the idea. 'Now, about religion—I see I have been given number five, which is Presbyterian. I am not, in fact, a Presbyterian.'

'What are you then?' said Mrs. Ellsmere.

Sheaffer paused. . . . Zen Buddhist with Trappist tendencies . . . no . . . better stick to the truth. . . . 'I don't believe in anything,' he said.

'Really,' said Mrs. Ellsmere.

'Really,' repeated Sheaffer.

'In that case,' said Mrs. Ellsmere, as if on the brink of a great discovery, 'you're an *atheist*.'

'No,' said Sheaffer, pursing his lips, 'not exactly. I don't believe in God, but I don't disbelieve in him.'

'In that case,' said Mrs. Ellsmere, 'you're an *agnostic*.'

'Not exactly that either,' said Sheaffer, a little uncertain about what an agnostic really was. 'You see, I'm prepared to give God a fair crack of the whip. If he wants to reveal himself to me, he can. If not, I'm not too bothered.'

'Well,' said Mrs. Ellsmere, 'we don't have anything here to fit you exactly. All I can suggest is "Unaffiliated" or "Other".'

'Very well,' said Sheaffer, 'I suppose it will have to be "Unaffiliated", although I don't really approve. I think it suggests I should be affiliated.'

' "Unaffiliated",' said Mrs. Ellsmere, 'it shall be.'

She handed the modified forms to Sheaffer, who signed them and handed them back. He thanked Mrs. Ellsmere and left the hall as quickly as possible.

It was almost dusk. Sheaffer walked past the Forester's Arms and glanced at the moving forms and colours and distorted faces behind the frosted glass of the latticed window. Social animals, he thought. . . . Pains in the arse . . . glad I make a stand . . . never dream of going in . . . How was your vac, John . . . arf arf arf . . . Oh Cannes is such a bore nowadays, Clive. . . . Lousy beer anyway . . . eighteen pence a pint . . . serves them right . . .

He smiled a superior-feeling smile and quickened his pace.
The Roaring Donkey, he thought. . . . Pint with the lads . . .
then dinner . . . with Suzie, if she comes . . . Think she will
. . . definitely . . . knows where her bread's buttered. . . .
Duck, I think . . . with roast potatoes . . . then some Turkish
coffee . . . or maybe China tea . . . used to like that . . . little
teapot . . . cup with a handle . . . not like last time . . . Velly
solly, no drinka China tea in cup wif handle. . . . Idiot . . .
sacked now probably . . . gone back to Hong Kong . . . what
do they call those boats again . . . pagodas . . . no, junks . . .
that's it, junks . . . sailing a junk again . . . smuggling opium
or such like . . . millions of them anyway . . . all with slit eyes
. . . Red Guards . . . rice, rice, and more rice . . . Rice with
Everything, by Who Flung Wesker . . . cream of rice soup
. . . roast beef and Yorkshire rice . . . a rice sandwich . . .
wonder what that tastes like . . .

'Sheaffer, Sheaffer,' someone shouted from across the
street.

Sheaffer looked across and waved, shouted, 'Hi, Rick,'
and walked on. . . . Nice guy, Rick . . . see him in the library
. . . not worth stopping though . . . nothing to say . . . Good
holiday? . . . Yes . . . and you? . . . Good to be back . . . Then
a painful silence . . . Glad he was on the other side . . . not
far now . . . Roaring Donkey . . . Mrs. Wilcox . . . hearty
laugh . . . like a man's . . . the usual, Sheaffer? . . . Sure . . .
nice big head on it . . . let some stick on your upper lip and
lick it with your tongue . . . taste the hops . . . mmmmmmmh . . .

Sheaffer opened the door of the Roaring Donkey. . . .
Empty . . . He walked into the back room of the lounge,
then returned to the lounge itself. . . . No one . . . He ambled
up to the small bar. The counter was sticky with spilled
beer; the gantry lights were turned off and the spirit bottles

hung with their attached jiggers in the half-gloom. He leaned across the bar, and, in his normal voice, said, 'Hello. Anyone around?' Then he raised his voice and repeated himself. Not a sound was heard.

. . . No one, absolutely no one . . . empty bar . . . unheard of . . . gone self-service . . . will be, anyway, in a few years . . . machines everywhere . . . press button . . . insert fifteen pence . . . press selection required . . . pull firmly . . . paper cups for everything . . . could help myself really . . . no . . . not done . . . so near and yet so far . . .

He walked over to the telephone on the wall. . . . 6 . . . 8 . . . 7 . . . 3 . . . *Bzzz* . . . *gnk* . . . Wonder what all these funny noises are . . . bet it's engaged . . . no . . . ringing one . . . two . . . three . . . come on . . . must be in . . . in the bath perhaps . . . no . . . no splashing . . . six . . . seven . . .

'Shit,' said Sheaffer aloud and slammed down the telephone.

. . . Still no one around . . . good . . . no one heard me. . . .

Then the front door opened and a strong-looking man with a face like a boxer's came into the Roaring Donkey. He walked past Sheaffer and rapped a coin on the bar.

'Service,' said the man in a gruff voice. 'Service.'

'There's no one there,' said Sheaffer.

'Ah cun see that fur maself, laddie,' said the fat man, looking disgusted.

'Okay,' said Sheaffer. 'I was only telling you.'

'Service. Give me sum bluddy service,' roared the fat man.

'I think we'll have to go somewhere else,' said Sheaffer.

'You,' said the fat man, 'cun go where ye fuckin' well like. Ah live next door and ah'm waiting till sum bugger serves me.'

Sheaffer decided to wait too.

The door opened again and a small man with a soft hat came in with a wife who was far too big for him. She sat down by the door.

'Whit wid ye like tae drink, ma dear?' said the small man.

'Och, Hector,' said the woman, 'Ah'll just huv a wee sherry.'

Hector walked jauntily up to the bar and turned to the fat man. ' 'Evenin'.'

' 'Evenin',' said the fat man. 'There's naebody there.'

'That's strange,' said Hector, 'very strange. How long have you been here?'

'Too fuckin' long,' said the fat man.

Hector's wife looked at the fat man in disgust, made a noise of disapproval in her throat, and folded her arms.

Sheaffer decided to phone again. . . . 6 . . . 8 . . . 7 . . . 3 . . . One . . . two . . .

Just then someone opened the door behind the bar and stepped in.

'Aboot bluddy time too,' said the fat man.

'Hello,' said Sheaffer.

'What's going on, who's calling?' said Suzie.

'Fur five fucking minutes,' said the fat man.

'Suzie,' said Sheaffer, 'it's Sheaffer, in the Roaring Donkey.'

'I huv been waitin' in this bluddy bar,' said the fat man.

'Who's with you?' said Suzie.

'No one, pet,' said Sheaffer. 'It's just a row behind. How about dinner tonight?'

'Do you, or do you not, want to be served?' said the barmaid.

'Great,' said Suzie, 'what time?'

'Of course I bluddy well do,' said the fat man.

'How about eight?' asked Sheaffer.

'Fine,' said Suzie, 'eight's fine.'

'I'm getting out of here, Hector,' said Hector's wife.

'I'll pick you up,' said Sheaffer.

'Are *you* coming, Hector?' said Hector's wife.

'Great,' said Suzie.

'Just a wee minute, dear,' said Hector.

'See you then,' said Sheaffer.

The bar door slammed. 'Wait,' shouted Hector.

' 'Bye,' said Suzie. Sheaffer put down the receiver.

'See whit ye've dun, ye great pilluck,' said Hector venomously to the fat man. 'The only bluddy time in the week I can get a drink and ye've driven hur oot with yer filthy tongue.'

The fat man lunged towards him, but Hector was out the door and away before he had gone two steps. The fat man growled and returned to his Guinness.

The barmaid looked very pale and shaken. Sheaffer smiled at her sympathetically. . . . Never seen her before . . . must be new . . . pretty though . . .

'Pint of special, please,' said Sheaffer. He took a stool. 'And could I have a thin glass, please?'

'Surely,' said the barmaid.

The fat man gulped the remainder of his Guinness voraciously and stalked out.

Pretty . . . very pretty . . . bit long in the nose though . . . nice hair . . . long . . . black . . . like long hair . . . bit greasy though . . . should use Starsilk with lanolin . . . for greasy hair . . . still, bit difficult asking for it . . . Excuse me, do you have anything for greasy hair? . . . Like asking for smoker's toothpaste . . . or contraceptives . . . much worse . . . Any particular make, sir? . . . God, no—anything, so long as it works . . . quickly though, before someone comes in . . . Good morning, Vicar . . . here are your contraceptives, Mr.

Sheaffer. . . . Good day, Vicar . . . Dropped my change all over the floor the first time too . . . best with machines . . . if they work . . . Excuse me, miss, I've just lost twenty pence in the contraceptive machine. . . .

'There,' said the barmaid, handing Sheaffer his glass. 'Twenty-two pence, please.'

'And twenty Gold Leaf, please,' said Sheaffer.

She turned and took a pack from the top of the gantry.

. . . Nice legs too . . . and thighs . . . perfect . . . thin ankles . . .

The barmaid handed him his cigarettes and took the folded pound note from Sheaffer's outstretched hand.

'Have one yourself,' he said.

'Thank you,' said the barmaid, 'I'll have a lager.' She took a bottle from the cooling shelf and poured the beer into a stemmed glass.

. . . Good . . . good . . . she took one . . . don't usually the first time . . . shy . . . wait until they know you better . . . or else they take the money . . . like to see them drink it . . . on the spot, if possible . . . chance for a chat . . .

'Thank you again,' said the barmaid. She took a small sip, rang up the total, and gave Sheaffer his change.

'You're new here, aren't you?' said Sheaffer, knowing perfectly well that she was.

'Yes,' said the girl. 'I started three weeks ago.'

'What's your name?'

'Beatrice,' said the girl.

. . . Pity about that . . . bad name . . . always imagine Beatrices with red faces . . . looks more like a Felicity or a Jane . . .

'I'm Sheaffer.'

'Is that your first name?' asked Beatrice.

'No,' said Sheaffer. 'It's my only name. You see, I was

born in Africa, miles from any church, so I never had a chance to be christened.'

Beatrice laughed. 'They must call you something,' she said.

'Just Sheaffer,' said Sheaffer. 'That suits me fine. Besides, it makes writing your name a lot easier.'

'What do you do, Sheaffer?' Beatrice asked, as she ran a fingernail gently around the rim of her glass.

'Oh, I'm a historian,' replied Sheaffer, as though historians were a rare and almost supernatural species.

'A historian of what?'

'Of sects,' said Sheaffer proudly.

'Oh!' said Beatrice, drawing back.

'Oh *no*,' said Sheaffer disdainfully, 'not *that*. *Sects*. You know, secret societies, religious groups, usually evil ones.'

'That must be fascinating,' said Beatrice, running the tip of her tongue lightly across the edge of her upper teeth.

'And what do you do, Beatrice?'

'Oh, I'm an occupational therapist—I just work here for extra money.'

'Really,' said Sheaffer, wondering what on earth an occupational therapist was. 'That must be fascinating.'

'It's very fulfilling work,' said Beatrice. She took the fat man's empty glass from the bar and began to wash it.

Sheaffer sipped his beer slowly. . . . God, occupational therapist . . . heard it somewhere before . . . posh name for a career adviser . . . no . . . therapy of some kind . . . massaging, I think . . . yes . . . She looks like a massager. . . . Wonder if she'll come out anyway . . . lovely girl . . . no wedding ring . . . or engagement . . . what is it again . . . second finger of left hand . . . or is it right . . . no . . . left . . . definitely not engaged . . .

'I was wondering, Beatrice,' said Sheaffer, as though a

great pronouncement was about to be made, 'if you would
like to come out for a drink with me sometime.'

'Oh, thank you,' said Beatrice without stopping to breathe.
'That would be just lovely.'

'How about Monday?'

'Lovely,' said Beatrice.

'Where do you live?'

'Ninety-three Woodland Road.'

'Fine,' said Sheaffer. 'I'll pick you up at nine, okay?'

'Okay,' said Beatrice.

The door opened and four workmen came in.

'Must go now, Beatrice,' said Sheaffer. 'See you Monday.'

' 'Bye.'

Sheaffer walked into the street. It was dark already. He
sighed, then smiled. Good start, he thought. There before
anyone else . . . pays to move fast . . . He smirked and lit a
cigarette, inhaling deeply, pleased with himself. Still, he
thought, strange she has no steady boy friend. . . . Jumped
at your offer quickly enough too . . . nothing wrong, I hope
. . . bad breath . . . or BO . . . no . . . or some hidden disfigure-
ment . . . or something wrong with her arse, like old Mrs.
Dalton in primary school . . . smelled like rotten fish . . .
grab the back seats, boys, here comes fishy Dalton . . . wonder if she's frigid . . . or a nympho . . . no . . . that wouldn't
put anyone off . . . just lonely, perhaps . . . needs friends . . .
no occupational therapists of her own age . . . good name,
that . . . occupational therapist . . . Good evening, Sir John,
allow me to introduce Beatrice, my occupational therapist . . .

Sheaffer smiled again. He reached his car and jumped in.
Time for a shower and a shave, a quick phone call home to
London, and then dinner. He pulled out from the kerb and
headed for Manor House.

2

MRS. MIRIAM WILCOX was the wife of Harold Wilcox, retired fireman, sometime professional wrestler, latterly publican and now sadly deceased, having fallen asleep one night over an unfinished pint of Campbell's extra-strong special brew and never waked up. Harold had lived most of his life in a state of suspended inebriation. Never drunk, yet never sober, he passed his days in the panacean nirvana between the two conditions, where all the problems of the world recede and the future holds nothing but promise. He had often joked of dying with a glass in his hand, and, in the final analysis, it was perhaps fitting that his flippant aspirations should have been fulfilled. Although he had been dead and gone a year, the patrons of the Roaring Donkey still spoke amongst themselves of Harold's dying with an unemptied glass before him as though it was somehow a testimony to the transcendental properties of ale. Mrs. Wilcox, a simple soul, had retained the glass and its contents and placed it in Harold's favourite room in their apartment above the Roaring Donkey. And every evening at seven she prayed assiduously for his soul and sprinkled some holy water from an empty Cologne bottle on the glass, and on Harold's favourite pipe, which lay beside it. Then she would sigh, wipe away a tear or two, and go to the kitchen for her dinner. On this particular Saturday, however—the anniversary of Harold's death—Mrs. Wilcox allowed herself a more considerable effusion than usual. She dispensed the holy water generously and then shuffled slowly into the kitchen with red-rimmed eyes and sat herself down at the shiny Formica-topped table.

'Oh, there, there, there,' said Beatrice comfortingly, hastening from the stove and laying her arm gently on Mrs. Wilcox's shoulder. 'What's wrong, Mrs. Wilcox?'

Mrs. Wilcox wept a bit more and wiped her eyes with a dirty handkerchief. 'It's Harold, dear,' she said, suppressing more tears. 'A year ago it was he went, and him only sixty and fine-looking for it too; and I do miss him so and hope that he's been spared.'

'He'll be fine,' said Beatrice soothingly, taking her arm from Mrs. Wilcox's shoulder and going back to stir the stew. 'It must be difficult, I know, but don't worry. I'm sure he's fine where he is.'

'Well,' said Mrs. Wilcox, 'it is worrying. You see, you never know if the Lord has decided to spare him—not that he was bad, you know, Beatrice. A good man he always was to me, even if he did swear and curse and blaspheme a bit and take a good drink and enjoy a fight from time to time. But he was a good man, my Harold, good to me and kind to those he liked.'

'What did he do before he came here?' asked Beatrice, bringing over the steaming stew and pouring some on Mrs. Wilcox's plate and some on her own.

'Oh, lovely, dear,' said Mrs. Wilcox, tasting the stew. 'Well, mmmmmmh, you see, he was, mmmmmmmh—this really is lovely stew, Beatrice—well, you see, Harold was a fireman and a wrestler—good at both of them, was my Harold. Once he beat Abdul the Hairy Sheik by two falls to one, although he broke a bone in his foot doing it.'

'Oh *really*!' said Beatrice, pretending to be much more impressed than she actually was. 'It's such a pity he didn't have a long retirement after all the work he did.'

Mrs. Wilcox paused to remove a sliver of boiled carrot from below her bottom dentures and continued, looking knowingly at Beatrice. 'You know how he died, Beatrice?' she asked.

'Oh no,' said Beatrice, who had been told how Harold Wilcox had died by every regular customer who came into the Roaring Donkey.

'In the bar itself,' said Mrs. Wilcox, holding back some more tears and dropping several marrowfat peas from her fork on to the floor. 'He died with a glass in his hand, Beatrice—the way he wanted to go. It was as if the Lord knew what my Harold wanted, Beatrice. And when his time came . . .'

'How awful,' said Beatrice with meaning. She closed her eyes briefly in a respectful gesture of sorrow, then added, 'I'm sure the Lord will take good care of him.'

'Well, it's Hell that I'm worried about,' said Mrs. Wilcox. 'You see, Harold changed to marry me—Catholic, you see —and he never . . . well . . . he never really embraced the church, quite. He had rows with the priest and never confessed and absolutely refused to kneel before the altar. And of course there were no last rites because, you understand, of the circumstances of his going. It was a Saturday night, you see, and we had cleared everything up, and my Harold and Ernie Green and Sheaffer were . . .'

'*Sheaffer*,' gasped Beatrice, amazed.

'Yes, Sheaffer,' said Mrs. Wilcox. 'Is he back yet? I haven't seen him since the beginning of the summer.'

'Yes—he's back,' said Beatrice. 'And he really was there, was he?'

'Oh yes,' said Mrs. Wilcox. 'Sheaffer and Ernie Green and my Harold used to play dominoes every Saturday night for hours and hours. Well, I was watching them, and Sheaffer said, "Come on, Harry"—yes, that was what he said, always called him "Harry"—and he said, "Come on, Harry, your turn," and my poor Harold just sat there looking like the beautiful man he was, with a smile across his face, and he still had that smile when they put him in the box, and he'll still have it to this very day, will my Harold.'

'What a dreadful shock,' said Beatrice, folding her napkin.

'Well, it was,' said Mrs. Wilcox, mopping up the thick gravy on her plate with a slice of bread. 'And I ran over and tried to waken him up but all he did was smile and look happy. The glass was in his hand, and could we get it from him? He wanted to take it with him, did my Harold, because he wasn't finished, you know. There was still some left. Loved his pint, my Harold. "Pint of Campbell's, Miriam," he used to say to me in the mornings, and then he'd take it to the toilet with him and drink it when he was on the bowl. Loved his beer, and it did him no harm, either. Good to me, he was—a beautiful man, and that was how he died.'

Beatrice thought hard of something consoling to say, but without success. However, Mrs. Wilcox was at no loss for words.

'Only one thing scared him,' she continued, revelling in finding someone new to reminisce to. 'The dentist. "I won't go, Miriam," he would say to me, and I used to say to him, "Now, Harold, you'll go and do as you're told," and I used to have to drag him there, and him with his big muscles shaking and his teeth chattering; and then when they put him under the gas he would say the most dreadful things about the dentist himself, and about the Catholic church and about Our Lady, and I'm only hoping that God has forgiven him, as I'm sure he has, because the poor man didn't know what he was saying.'

'What about Sheaffer?' asked Beatrice. 'Did he come here really often?'

'Every Saturday,' said Mrs. Wilcox, 'he came, and if he had a girl with him, she stayed too, and we all played dominoes except for me. Good at dominoes, Sheaffer—good at everything, Sheaffer. Made all the funeral arrangements, so he did, and sent a wreath and read a bit at the service. And on the wreath he said, the dear boy—because I remember it to this day and always will—"To my dear friend, Harry Wilcox, who lived and died as I would choose to live and die." '

'What else do you know about Sheaffer?' asked Beatrice, trying hard not to sound too interested, but not making a very good job of it.

'You know him, do you?'

Beatrice nodded.

'I don't know all that much about him,' said Mrs. Wilcox in reply. 'Strange boy, Sheaffer, but one of the best. No first name, you know—just Sheaffer.'

'Just Sheaffer,' repeated Beatrice.

'And you know he studies sects,' said Mrs. Wilcox.

'Yes, he told me.'

'And that he's very rich.'

'*No*,' gasped Beatrice.

'You mean,' said Mrs. Wilcox, pouring herself a cup of tea, 'that you haven't heard of Sheaffer toothpaste?'

'Not *that* Sheaffer!' said Beatrice disbelievingly.

'His father founded it,' said Mrs. Wilcox, 'but he doesn't do anything except read the papers and watch television, and sometimes play golf, or table tennis if he has the energy. Half of the business is in Sheaffer's name, but he doesn't want anything to do with it. Just wants to study sects— that's what he told me. Funny, I thought it was sex he said the first time—hahahahaha. But our Sheaffer has no interest in toothpaste. Ten million tubes a day they sell all over the world, and the lad uses Colgate himself. Told my Harold and me, so he did, that we could have as much of it as we wanted, but, of course, we both had false teeth. So he gave us Sheaffer Denture Cream instead, but I still use a glass of water with some baking soda in it; keeps them cleaner, but don't tell him that, or he might get upset.'

'Actually—he asked me out,' said Beatrice, rising and taking her dirty plate to the sink. 'I rather like him.'

'Oh, then he'll take you to the Grange,' said Mrs. Wilcox confidently. 'But if you go out with him often, he'll insist you come here. Even when he went out with Lord Dundas's daughter, Lady Gwendoline, the Maid of Drumkinnes, he brought her into the Roaring Donkey every Saturday night. He likes his girls to see him as he really is, you know, in his favourite surroundings; doesn't like going to fancy places unless it's really necessary.'

'What was *she* like—the daughter, I mean, of Lord Dundas?' asked Beatrice, trying to sound as unconcerned as possible.

'Beautiful,' said Mrs. Wilcox, with her customary tactlessness. 'Beautiful girl, but she knew it. They were engaged, you know—funny business. Don't know what happened. Or the other time.'

'Other time,' said Beatrice, 'what other time?'

'Oh, he's been engaged twice, has our Sheaffer,' said Mrs. Wilcox. 'Twice. Strange, you know. Can't imagine anyone turning down our Sheaffer. Still'—she paused—'perhaps he turned them down when it came to the bit. Strange though. I don't know really.'

'Well,' said Beatrice, feeling a little weak at the knees, 'I . . . I'd best be getting back to work now.'

'Fine, dear,' said Mrs. Wilcox, wiping her nose with the back of her hand. 'Lovely meal. Ever so glad you came to work here.'

3

FATHER SCRAW ate as much of the burning curry as his mouth could stand; then he separated the shrimps from what remained, chewed them with his rotten teeth, and savoured them on his tongue until one found its way into a particularly rotten tooth. He shut his eyes, twitched his nose, and softly moaned, but not softly enough to escape the acute hearing of his wife. From across the candles in the silver candelabrum that she had imagined to be French sixteenth century but that was in fact Hong Kong twentieth century, Winifred Scraw glared at her priestly husband with owl-like eyes on bulging promontories set into a face that might have resulted from crossbreeding a giraffe and an ageing bulldog.

'*Well*, Rupert,' she said, as if he had committed a sin against the Holy Ghost, 'and what may I ask is wrong *this* time?'

'Nothing, dear,' said Father Scraw, extracting the offending shrimp from the decaying molar cavity with his fingers. 'It was just . . .'

'Oh, Rupert—do you always have to be so vulgar at table, picking your teeth and suchlike?'

'Really, dear,' said Father Scraw, trying to be patronising and falling far short of it, 'in the highest court circles even lords and ladies pick their teeth. So I don't see why . . .'

'Oh, Rupert,' said Mrs. Scraw, 'sometimes I just wonder why I married you.'

And I sometimes wonder, dear, why I did . . .

'How anyone can behave themselves so badly at table . . .'

Oh, to pick my teeth when I want to pick them . . .

'. . . when he should be a *leader* in the community.'

Oh, for peace and quiet and a pipe of rich dark honey-dew . . .

There was a charged silence broken only by the ticks of the grandfather clock by the door.

'It was simply too hot, Winifred,' said Father Scraw courageously. 'And you *know* I can't eat hot curries.'

'Three hours, I spent,' said Winifred Scraw, subduing her voice so that she might raise it again. 'Three hours I slaved over a hot stove to make that curry for you. "What do you want, Rupert?" I asked you. "Curry, my dear," you said. And what do I get? "Too hot", "too tough", "too tender". It's always what I get, Rupert—complaints, complaints, and more complaints about this, that and the next thing.' She leered across the table and continued, 'What you want, Rupert, is a cook, and not a wife.'

Bloody right, I do, thought Father Scraw.

'You want someone to do your dirty work for you, Rupert, that's it.'

You've always managed to keep your hands pretty clean anyway. . . .

'And you know something, Rupert—you just don't deserve me.'

Who does, my dear? Who does? . . .

'Really, dear,' said Father Scraw, exasperated.

'You, Rupert, deserve nothing but a whore.'

'Come, come, dear,' said Father Scraw, thinking that it might not be such a bad idea after all, 'that's a bit strong now, isn't it?'

'No, Rupert, it certainly is not,' said Mrs. Scraw, whose

eyes looked, as they did periodically, about to fall out. 'When I consider the hours I've spent cooking . . .'

'Of all your many attributes, my dear Winifred,' said Father Scraw, slowly, deliberately, and bravely, 'cooking has never really been your "forte", as it were, now has it?'

'*What?*'

'Cooking, my dear,' repeated Father Scraw, enjoying her utter astonishment, 'the preparation of food by the application of heat. You've always overdone the "heat" aspect of it, my dear. It's inconceivable, in fact, that anything you make can be eaten at once. I sometimes think that you even resent salads, simply because you can't spice them up and put them in the oven.'

'Oooooooooh!' gasped Mrs. Scraw, who was about to say that she was speechless but was too speechless to say it.

'Anyway, I must go now,' said Father Scraw, rising from the table. 'Must call Sheaffer—been a mix-up about the altar wine.'

'Sheaffer,' repeated Mrs. Scraw, who disapproved of Sheaffer enough to recover her voice in time to run him down. 'That disgusting boy who doesn't have a first name and smokes those foul cigarettes and drinks all of your Madeira when he comes over here, and . . .'

'There's nothing disgusting about him at all, Winifred,' said Father Scraw firmly. 'He just has his own . . .'

'Don't tell me, Rupert. I *know*. Don't say a word about that boy. I heard him telling you a disgusting story once, and you laughed, Rupert; I heard him tell you in the vestry and you laughed, louder, I think, than I have ever heard you laugh before, although I was only walking past outside the door. And it was disgusting, Rupert, positively plebeian.'

'What was the joke, dear?' asked Father Scraw, enjoying himself. 'I don't remember the occasion.'

'Oh, Rupert,' she replied, heaving and sighing, 'it was carnal—positively lewd. He has a mind like a stinking sewer, that Sheaffer—a stinking sewer—and frankly, Rupert, your own mind isn't much better.'

'I still don't remember that joke. I'm sure it's just your imagination, Winifred.'

'You *know* what joke I mean, Rupert. It was disgusting and you laughed. They could have heard you laughing at the bottom of the High Street if they'd wanted to. It was one of these intercourse jokes about prostitutes and whores and licentious men, and you laughed, Rupert—a man of God, and you laughed. And any person who tells jokes like that should be . . .'

'Oh, I remember now,' said Father Scraw, starting to chuckle.

'Ooooooooh, Rupert, sometimes I just . . .'

But Father Scraw had had enough. 'See you later, dear,' he said as he walked through the door and breathed the serene and pure air of the hall, free from the hot curry smells. The day's ordeal is over, he thought, and a calm and un-eventful evening lies ahead. He lit his pipe and sucked at the rich dark honeydew mixture, and smiled as he thought of smoking it in front of the fire in the vestry with his shoes off and his feet up and the warm glow from the coal deliciously hot on his trousered legs. He picked up the final copy of the *Sports Gazette* from beneath the door and went off to scrutinise the football results.

Sheaffer was sitting in the toilet wondering whether or not the Queen got her toilet paper free or had to pay for it like everyone else, when Father Scraw telephoned. He wiped himself with alacrity, tugged open the bathroom door, and pulled up his trousers as he edged his way to the telephone and reached it on the fifth ring.

'Hello.'

'Ah, Sheaffer.'

'Father Scraw.'

'Yes. Not disturbing you, I hope.'

' 'Fraid so,' said Sheaffer. 'You caught me on the bowl.'

'Oh *no*—ever so sorry,' said Father Scraw, sounding very sorry. 'Do you . . . well . . . want to . . . What I mean is . . . were you finished?'

'Oh, yes,' replied Sheaffer. 'I was just thinking. Pondering, you know—good place for a ponder, the old bowl. You don't happen to know if the Queen gets her toilet paper free?'

'What?'

'The Queen,' repeated Sheaffer. 'Does she pay for her own toilet tissue?'

'Never thought about it,' said Father Scraw, cackling into the receiver.

'Well,' continued Sheaffer, 'you know that businesses make goods by appointment to the Queen—purveyors of this, that, and the next thing. Well, maybe there's a purveyor of toilet paper.'

'Could be,' said Father Scraw. 'Wonder what kind she uses.'

'Something soft for the royal bum,' said Sheaffer. 'Anyway, what can I do for you, Father?'

'It's about the altar wine, Sheaffer.'

'Yes.'

'Well, it's not altar wine at all.'

'Lord,' said Sheaffer. 'What is it?'

'Where did you get it from?'

'Hepburn's Warehouses. They sell everything there. I just asked for two cases of the best altar wine.'

'Well,' said Father Scraw ominously, 'someone has deceived you.'

'What is it then?'

'Books.'

'Good Lord—God no . . . It's not . . . well, you know.'

'Yes.'

'Imported?'

'Yes.'

'Swedish?'

'Right again.'

'Oh good God, Father,' said Sheaffer. 'And I thought just that when I put them down on the floor in the store this afternoon. They were the only thing I had ever seen in wrappings like that except contraceptives.'

'Oh, there's some of them too.'

'Lord! Imported too?'

'Yes. The writing on the packet is in Swedish, but I think the general principle is much the same.'

'Look,' said Sheaffer, 'I'm really incredibly sorry about this, Father. I had no idea that . . .'

'Don't worry about it, Sheaffer.'

'But what if one of the Women's Guild was to come across them?'

'Oh, I've taken them up to the attic,' said Father Scraw, sounding as if he had the situation very much under control.

'I'm sure you haven't looked at them, Father, but . . . well . . . what sort . . .'

'Oh, I have.'

'A . . . are they disgusting?'

'Some of them are filthy, some are filthier, and some are the filthiest things I've ever seen in all my life.'

36

'So you've had a pretty good look at them then?'

'Well, after all,' said Father Scraw, 'the Swedes are our brethren, and it would be wrong of us not to try to understand their problems.'

'Especially when we have two boxloads,' said Sheaffer. 'Look, Father, I'll take them back next week and get the real thing.'

'Nonsense,' said Father Scraw. 'My assistant can go to Edinburgh for more wine. I think we should hang on to these, for the present, at least.'

'In the attic?'

'Yes,' replied Father Scraw.

'Are you *sure* it's safe?'

'Absolutely. No one has been up there for years, and I've covered them up with sackcloth. Would have used some ashes too—hahahahaha—but couldn't find any. Oh dear— bad joke—hahahaha.'

'Good show,' said Sheaffer. 'Once again, I'm really sorry.'

'Don't be. Now, can you come to lunch tomorrow? Then I can show you afterwards what the awful man sold you by mistake.'

'Well . . .'

'You really ought to witness the extent of this wretched man's duplicity, Sheaffer.'

'Well, I'd love to, but . . .'

'My sister is cooking.'

'Cynthia? Oh, I'd love to come.'

'Yes, Cynthia,' said Father Scraw. 'She's doing it to give Winifred a break and ourselves a treat. Maybe we'll get something we can eat, for a change.'

'Great—what time?'

'Twelve o'clock. Hendricks, the preacher at the morning service, will be there.'

'Damn—I won't be able to make the sermon.'

'Oh, don't worry about that,' said Father Scraw. 'I'll write out a short guide to what he said and you can pretend you were there.'

'Good man,' said Sheaffer. 'Well, I'd best go now, Father. I have a little work to do before dinner.'

'See you tomorrow,' said Father Scraw. ' 'Bye.'

Sheaffer got up and made himself a stiff drink. He sat down in front of the television set to watch a programme called 'Angling in the Japanese Backwaters', which intrigued him because of its title, and while it was going on he decided he would not pay even a brief visit to the Roaring Donkey that night, because it would be busy and he wouldn't have much time to talk to Beatrice, since he was eating at eight and, anyway, he was so taken with her already that he wanted to preserve the illusion so that he could think of her beatifically over the weekend.

In his sprawling, yieldingly comfortable armchair, he then began to read about the atrocities committed on the Albigensian heretics by their persecutors—his favourite and principal research topic. He felt better after that because he had done some work and had also enjoyed reading the vivid descriptions of the carnage in old French. He called his mother next and learned more about his father's sleep-walking and his tendencies towards Roman Catholicism; he was relieved to discover that both conditions were giving less cause for concern than during the previous week. Then he shaved and listened to some music. He ran a bath, immersed himself in the tub, and did a bit of bathtub philosophising about love. When the water became lukewarm, he turned on the hot tap and sank back with only his head above the surface. Like many men, Sheaffer felt exceedingly important in his bath; and so he pretended he was a sports announcer on the radio describing the cup final, in which he had just scored the winning goal for the team that he founded, financed, managed, captained, and had taken from the fourth division to the first in three seasons.

Then he was the announcer of the B B C News. . . . Good evening . . . Confusion in Westminster today . . . The Prime Minister, Lord Cluff Puff, has resigned. . . . The Queen has asked Lord Sheaffer to form a government. . . . Will you be relinquishing your title, Lord Sheaffer? . . . Naturally . . . Crowds gathered outside Downing Street in the late afternoon . . . We want Sheaffer! We want Sheaffer! We want Sheaffer! . . . Let them eat cake. . . .

Today, Her Majesty the Queen asked me to form the next government. . . . I have accepted the task, hard though it may be. . . . Father Scraw will be the next Archbishop of Canterbury. . . . Mrs. Wilcox, Minister for Strong Drink . . . Suzie Elliot, Minister in Charge of Voluptuous Affairs . . . and Beatrice . . . ah yes, the beautiful Beatrice . . . Occupational Therapist to the Prime Minister and First Massager of the Treasury. . . . She will also, of course, be in charge of selling the new state newspaper—*Der Sheaffer*. . . . Yes . . . good idea . . . Lord, this water's getting cold. . . . And the time . . . dear Jesus . . . seven-thirty . . .

Sheaffer splashed quite a bit as he hastened from the bath. He dried himself, dressed, looked in the mirror, and decided that he was much more handsome than even he had previously considered. He gave himself a knowing look and a big wink, told himself aloud that the night was young, and waved the mirror good-bye. Only when he reached the lift did he realise he had forgotten to brush his teeth; so he sucked a peppermint toffee instead, just to make sure his breath smelled reasonably fresh.

4

SUSAN ELLIOT lived on the corner of Sebastopol Crescent in a whitewashed fisherman's cottage which her mother had bought from the fisherman and given her for her twenty-first birthday. Susan's mother was a shrewd businesswoman, unlike Susan's father, who, after many years of tottering on the brink, had finally become a confirmed alcoholic. He had married Susan's mother mainly for her money and partly because she was going to have Susan. When Mrs. Elliot realised what a lazy good-for-nothing her husband was, she began divorce proceedings against him, and the divorce was just about to come through. Mr. Elliot now spent his days in the East End of London, where he was a familiar sight in the local bars. Susan's mother had remained in Lindenlee and had invested all her money in a Georgian mansion. Then she had converted the Georgian mansion into a hotel, the Georgian, and made thousands of pounds every year from American tourists who believed in things like 'paying for atmosphere' and who arrived with sunglasses and cigars and hundreds of dollars and departed with tartan ties, bonnets, kilts, miniature bagpipes, paperback editions of Burns, dreadful nose colds, and some loose change.

Susan's mother had given Susan everything she wanted, except, of course, a father. True, she had received offers of marriage from eligible men, but her divorce had taken a long time to reach the courts, largely because Mr. Elliot kept changing the bars he frequented and was difficult to locate; and, in any case, Mrs. Elliot found in time that a variety of bedfellows, old and young, best satisfied her sexual and emotional desires. Many highly respected and some not-so-respected men from Lindenlee and its university had spent torrid nights in the Georgian, and if Susan's mother had ever turned to blackmail, she could have spent the remainder of her days in the Bahamas. Susan herself would not have been a student at Lindenlee but for the intervention of her mother, who knew her daughter's academic limitations and had seduced the Dean of Arts at a coffee-morning on the day the Admissions Board met. Consequently, for the past two years, despite a high failure rate in her examinations, Susan had been allowed to resume her studies on health grounds, although she had never been sick a day in her life and frequently went for walks in the country instead of going to classes.

Susan was sexually almost insatiable; still, she was a normal girl in many ways. She enjoyed cooking and sewing and gossiping and watching television and reading love stories in women's magazines. She had good taste in clothes, applied make-up sparingly and tastefully, and could arrange her long dark-brown hair stunningly in any number of ways. She was around five feet tall and had huge wild blue eyes and long eyelashes, a small nose, and a rather-too-big mouth with lips that were deliciously curved and moulded, and eminently kissable. She had sharply defined cheekbones, and soft, almost unblemished smooth skin. Her waist was slender, but not so slender that she wasn't cosy to cuddle. Her legs looked delicate, and neatly tapered to thin, almost brittle-seeming ankles and small feet. But her distinctive feature was her breasts—large, fully formed, and shaped to perfection—which she often showed to advantage in tantalis-

41

ingly low-cut dresses. And she was pulling a particularly tan-
talising dress over her head when Sheaffer knocked on the
door.

'Oh dear God,' she muttered, then raised her voice. 'Is
that you, Sheaffer?'

'Are you expecting someone else then?' came the voice of
Sheaffer from behind the closed door. 'It's bloody cold out
here; let me in, for God's sake.'

Suzie walked to the door, with her dress hanging loosely
around her, and opened it.

'Sheaffer! Oh, Sheaffer—what beautiful flowers,' she
said, clutching the bunch of roses that Sheaffer thrust into
her hand. 'Oh, Sheaffer, darling, I'm going to give you the
biggest kiss. . . .'

'Well, let me get inside first, Suzie, dear,' said Sheaffer,
who enjoyed long passionate kisses but enjoyed them more
indoors.

'How have you been then?' she asked, moving close to
him.

'Mmmmmmh.' He kissed her in a way that he hoped
would appear passionate, eased her across to the sofa, took
her face between his hands, and pressed his lips even harder
against hers; then he eased the limp red silky dress from
her shoulders and halfway down her arms, ran his hand
slowly across the soft warm fleshy curves of her breasts,
and felt her thighs beneath him rubbing frantically against
him as she drew up her dress, opened her legs, and pressed
against him harder and harder, reaching for his partial erection with her other hand. Suddenly he stopped; he extricated
himself with difficulty from the tangle and sat on the side of
the sofa; his tie hung limply over his shoulder; he smelled
the warmth of her body, the expensive perfume; he watched
the heat in her face, the frantic movements of her body, the

pale-blue patterns of the cushions highlighting her white thighs.

'I could do with a drink, Suzie,' he said.

'Jesus, don't stop now!' She stretched quickly across for the zip of his fly, but Sheaffer, who knew her technique backwards, turned deftly at the last moment and walked over to a chair by the television set.

'Gin, I think,' he said. 'Some tonic if you have it.'

'You never will do it,' she said bitterly, quivering a little and slightly tearful. 'You'll kiss me, but you'll never make love.'

'It's not making love,' said Sheaffer. 'As I've told you before, it's screwing.'

'Oh, don't use that horrible word.'

'Actually, it's a very apt term,' Sheaffer said. 'You screw someone for the sake of a good screw. You make love to someone you're in love with. Now, I'm not in love with you, and I'm not going to screw you because I'm not a sexual mechanic. You know what you need, of course—a bloody machine to keep you going all day.'

'Sometimes,' Suzie said softly, 'I think you hate me.'

'That's why I bring you roses,' said Sheaffer, 'because of my great loathing for you.'

'Ooooooh, Sheaffer—sometimes I want to murder you. You lead me on and then you . . . God! . . . But they are lovely, lovely roses.'

'Come on,' said Sheaffer, winking to her and taking his drink from her outstretched hand, 'get dressed. Then we can go and eat. I'm starved.'

'Oh, all right,' she replied, sighing, shrugging her shoulders, and walking, disgruntled, into the bedroom. Sheaffer sank back into the armchair and closed his eyes. His erection had completely subsided. He felt a little cheap, wondered why, then knew why, knew he had been cheap, and so stopped wondering why as an instinctive means of defence. God, he thought. . . . Sex, sex, sex . . . all of us . . . obsessed, obsessed . . . everyone . . . men . . . women . . . birds . . . goats . . . horses . . . fish . . . Wonder how they do it, the fish . . . back to the breeding grounds . . . no . . . breeding waters . . . Banging away all the time . . . sexual urge . . . me too . . . just as bad . . . used to carry them everywhere . . . prophylactics . . . just in case I banged into something nice . . . packet of three . . . screw, screw, and more screw . . . As for her . . . Jesus . . . at it all the time . . . take anything, she will . . . big dicks . . . little dicks . . . white dicks . . . black dicks . . . yellow dicks . . . Suppose they must have yellow ones . . . the Chinese . . . and the Japanese . . . and the Koreans . . . Take anything, her . . . pathetic really . . . insatiable lust . . . Lovely, though . . . most beautiful breasts in the world . . . told her that once . . . but not my type . . . no love . . . not got the energy anyway . . . wants it all day . . . before breakfast even . . . I think . . . couldn't keep up the pace . . . Want someone quiet . . . peaceful . . . loving . . . affectionate . . . compassionate . . . kind . . . beautiful . . . intelligent . . . good teeth . . .

'Have you used that toothpaste yet, Suzie?'

'It's awful,' said Suzie, from the bedroom. 'Tastes like bananas.'

'That's because it's banana-flavoured,' said Sheaffer.

'I asked for cherry flavour.'

'Oh, damn. Then I must have given it to Abdul, and he hates cherries. How is he, anyway?'

'Ill.'

'What?'

'A cold,' said Suzie, emerging from the bedroom. 'Okay, I'm ready. Come on.'

'Of course, they don't have colds in India, do they?' said Sheaffer. 'Must be like us catching yellow fever, them getting a cold.'

'Come on,' said Suzie. 'You were the one that wanted to move.'

'I'm not so hungry now,' said Sheaffer. 'I've been thinking about sex.'

'One day,' said Suzie, 'you might get round to finding out what it's like.'

'Oh, I know what it's like,' said Sheaffer. 'But at least when I do it it's not like just having a cigarette.'

'Whoever said it was?' she said, opening the door; Sheaffer groped for his car keys as she closed it firmly behind them.

The remains of what had once been a sprightly young duck stood between them on the blood-red tablecloth. The napkin in Sheaffer's fingers was coated with thick grease.

'Good duck,' he said to the dangling waiter as he brought them Turkish coffee. He flicked his napkin on to his side plate as if it were a lump of faeces.

'How's your mother, Suzie?'

'Having an affair with Professor Ramsbottom,' she replied with facetious disdain. 'You know, the civil war expert. He haunts the Georgian in his pyjamas.'

'I should think he looks awful in his pyjamas.'

'Oh, Mother doesn't care about that. You see, it's his mind she's in love with. You see, she has a crush on Rupert of the Rhine, and Ramsbottom's writing a book on him —the world's leading expert in the field.'

Sheaffer felt an uncomfortable stickiness on his spine; the restaurant was stiflingly hot.

'Speaking of books,' he continued, without much enthusiasm, 'read any good ones lately?'

'Some Henry Miller,' Suzie replied, wiping some roast-duck juices from her lips, and licking them.

'Oh yes,' said Sheaffer, in a voice of great authority, '*Death of a Salesman*.'

'No—that's *Arthur*.'

'Are you *quite* sure?' said Sheaffer, eyeing her suspiciously.

'Definitely,' she replied. 'Are we ready to leave? I don't really want this coffee.' Sheaffer took a pound note from his pocket, handed it to Suzie, and had a token sip of his coffee out of loyalty to the waste-not-want-not maxims his mother had taught him.

'What's *that* for?' she asked, looking at the crisp new pound note in amazement.

'The tip.'

'Just leave it on the table.'

'Oh, it's just that I don't want to leave it,' said Sheaffer. 'You see, I don't approve of tipping—suggests they're inferior.'

'But they are.'

'Ah, but that's not the point, Suzie,' said Sheaffer, rising to pay the bill. 'We shouldn't think of them that way.'

'Jesus!'

'We'll talk about him later,' said Sheaffer.

Suzie wanted to go to a party; Sheaffer did not like parties, except his own, or ones at which he was considered to be indispensable to the proceedings. However, they went to a party.

The party was at Crumpton Lodge, an old Victorian house with high ceilings and large rooms, and stairs that always looked to be falling down but never did. The host of the party was called MacTaggart, and MacTaggart held several parties a year. MacTaggart had few acquaintances and fewer friends, so he held parties regularly in the hope that his circle would grow and prosper. Unfortunately for MacTaggart, this did not happen; he was a very affected person with an exaggerated sense of his own sporting abilities, and he was always complaining that he had not been selected to play in soccer matches which, had he been at a larger university than Lindenlee, he would never have been considered for anyway. MacTaggart also told the same boring jokes over and over again, mostly about himself and how he had duped people in positions of authority; he was really rather a pathetic creature. MacTaggart had, however, one great redeeming feature which rendered all his limitations bearable for a concise period of time, and that was the fact that his father, Rudolf MacTaggart, owned the largest distillery in Scotland. Consequently, although the company at his parties was rarely memorable, it was usually possible to forget this shortly after arriving at them.

Sheaffer took Suzie's coat to a first-floor bedroom in MacTaggart's huge house. There were no more than four coats already on the bed; MacTaggart's party had not, it seemed, been well advertised.

'Why, Sheaffer, old son,' said MacTaggart himself, emerging from the dancing area with a glass of Scotch gripped in his left hand, 'how good to see you again.'

'Good to see you too, MacTaggart,' replied Sheaffer with insincere but convincing enthusiasm.

'And you *too*, Suzie,' continued MacTaggart, peering lovingly at her plunging neckline. 'Did you meet anyone else on the way here?' he inquired hopefully. Sheaffer and Suzie shook their heads. At that moment MacTaggart would have welcomed a hundred beggars at his door and feasted them on broiled swan and green Chartreuse.

MacTaggart led them into a huge room, darkly lit with blue and orange light bulbs. In the far corner, an employee of the Lindenlee Mobile Disco Unit was sorting out popular records and labouring under the misapprehension that people would soon be dancing to them. MacTaggart poured Sheaffer and Suzie a full glass of Scotch each.

'Cheers,' said MacTaggart with spirit.

'Cheers,' they replied in unison.

Sheaffer glanced around. There were five other people standing in the vast room, including the host himself; they bore themselves uncomfortably, each of them hoping that people would arrive soon to relieve them from more of Mac-Taggart's awful, boring, predictable, repetitive jokes. Four of them were male. The only girl present, apart from Suzie, was about eighteen, grotesquely fat; thick folds of flab hung from her body in slices.

'My sister,' said MacTaggart, introducing the girl to Sheaffer and Suzie. 'Sheaffer is a toothpaste magnate, Ronalda,' he added, and then moved quickly over to the door to tell two 'friends' another favourite joke.

'Are you really?' gasped Ronalda, as if the Shah of Iran had just asked for her hand in marriage. 'And you *know* Claude?'

'Claude?'

'Claude,' repeated Ronalda, almost indignantly, and indignation had never worn well on her. 'My brother—Claude!' And she pointed to MacTaggart with a podgy index finger.

'Oh, MacTaggart—oh *yes*,' said Sheaffer, considering humility but rejecting it in favour of burlesque. 'Known him for years.' He sipped his Scotch.

MacTaggart asked Suzie to dance. 'Just to start things off,' he said. They took to the floor and, on MacTaggart's instructions, the hired disc jockey began to play 'Some Enchanted Evening'.

Just then MacTaggart's lonely French tutor arrived, looking starched and drawn and uncomfortably well dressed. Sheaffer poured him a very large drink, and introduced him to Ronalda, who smiled a mouthful of capped teeth; they began to talk about the long-range weather forecast. Sheaffer walked to the door, watching, out of the corner of his eye, MacTaggart contorting his body into strange unrhythmic shapes in an attempt to be fashionable.

Two girls arrived, muscular types, bred on the land and immediately recognisable as competitors in low-grade equestrian events; the type who always knocked the first fence down.

'Where's Claude?' asked one of the girls as if she were seeking an audience with the Pope.

'Dancing,' said Sheaffer, pointing to the isolated couple on the floor. 'Can I get you a drink?'

'Oh, I don't drink,' said the girl.

'Nor do I,' said her friend, very properly.

'Fair enough,' said Sheaffer, smiling and patting himself on the chest. 'All the more for us.'

The muscular girls did not think this remark was very funny. One of them looked disapprovingly at Sheaffer's floral tie.

'Some Enchanted Evening' scraped to an end. MacTaggart and Suzie sat down; then MacTaggart went to the bathroom to comb his hair, which had become dishevelled from vigorous gyrations. Suddenly there was a bright flash; the machine had played its last tune of the evening and in its demise had thwarted MacTaggart's French tutor, who had just summoned up enough courage to ask the flabby Ronalda to dance.

'Here's good old Tom,' someone said, as an anaemic youth with a face like an elongated isosceles triangle marched slowly into the room looking as miserable as sin.

'Fucking cold out here,' said good old Tom, who still got a thrill out of swearing in public after years of parental repression. The muscular girls looked aghast.

'Come and dance, Tom,' said Suzie, who felt that with the right training much might be made of Tom.

'Fucking good idea,' said Tom, in best BBC English.

'The machine's broken,' said the disc jockey disgustedly.

'Lord, no,' moaned MacTaggart, returned from his hair-combing, 'the party's ruined.'

'Not quite ruined,' said Sheaffer, looking mischievously at four dozen bottles of Glen MacTaggart malt whisky on a nearby table.

'We could always tell stories,' said MacTaggart, cheering up. 'I have several new ones, and, of course, there are all the old favourites.'

There was an unhappy silence; everyone felt very sorry for MacTaggart; no one felt it would be kind to leave, obviously; no one could leave unnoticed; and no one really felt entitled to another drink without doing something for it.

'Why don't we play horsey-horsey?' said Ronalda.

No one knew how to play horsey-horsey except good old Tom, and it needed six people to play. MacTaggart decided to fill up everyone's glass with ridiculously generous measures in order to limit departures to an absolute minimum. The French tutor was already swaying from his first Scotch; he began to sing songs softly in French and made circular motions with his left foot, which didn't help his balance any.

'What a wonderful voice,' said an enthralled Ronalda.

Everyone sat around in a circle on the floor to listen to the French tutor, who was gaining confidence all the time. Suzie curled up to Sheaffer's shoulder. The disc jockey was fiddling around aimlessly with a screwdriver, coating himself with oil, and occasionally mumbling compound swear words in a loud imprecise voice. The French tutor sang five more songs and then passed out. Someone phoned for a taxi to take him home. The whisky flowed. Ronalda recited a few poems about animals that she had learned by heart. No one listened, but everyone continued to drink. Tom told a humorous story about his travels in Burma, and Ronalda plumped herself down on the floor, her massive rubbery bum spreading out like a sagging barrage balloon. Then MacTaggart, having filled everyone's glass once more, told a few stories about his triumphs over bureaucracy, which everyone laughed at heartily. When he had finished, everyone who was capable of patting him on the back got up and did so. During all this time no one else arrived: the Scotch bottles stood looking disappointedly over the sparse collection of partakers. The disc jockey went home to bed. The two muscular girls thanked MacTaggart for a wonderful evening, and MacTaggart thanked them for coming.

Sheaffer sipped his ninth Scotch; Suzie, half asleep, tickled his tummy.

'Must be Sunday, now,' she whispered drowsily.

Sheaffer looked at his watch; 1.00 a.m. He cradled the Scotch glass lovingly in his hand. 'Sunday,' he repeated softly, almost under his breath. 'And we both know one thing, Suzie. *Nothing*, absolutely *nothing*, ever happens on Sunday.'

Sunday

I

SHEAFFER did not feel very well on Sunday morning. As
he wound his way down Carpenter Street he sensed a dreadful uncertainty as to where his next step would take him. A
cannon ball seemed to be suspended somewhere inside the
top of his head, round about where his brain should be, and,
as he walked, the cannon ball was slowly moving around and
occasionally banging against one side or the other. As he
crossed the junction with Ascott Lane, church bells began
to ring; the cannon ball effect increased; an Austin pulled
up sharply in front of him, and the irate driver uttered aud-
ible obscenities in his direction, but Sheaffer could not think
of anything unpleasant enough to say to the driver and con-
tented himself with making a very obscene gesture with his
fingers. A middle-aged woman in the passenger seat gasped
and said, 'Oh, Walter,' but Walter must have been feeling
rather like Sheaffer was feeling that morning and he drove
on without further ado.

Sheaffer paused outside Logan's General Stores, and then
stood in the doorway looking at synthetic flavoured bones
for dogs in three different sizes. . . . Fido . . . the new synthetic bone . . . your dog just won't know the difference . . .
mutton flavour . . . pork flavour . . . beef flavour . . . God . . .
what next? . . . Here, boy . . . good dog . . . 'at's a boy . . .
come and eat your plastic bone . . . you just won't know the
difference . . . Everyone everywhere is eating Fido . . . the

new plastic bone . . . Suppose you can use it again and again . . . yes . . . thought so . . . says it on the packet . . . Poor dog . . . crunching away at the bloody thing and never getting anywhere . . . Wish I had a decent bone again . . . not like these awful plastic things . . . something to get my teeth into . . . Perhaps I'll try a human bone . . . And, of course, then they'll start eating us . . . and who came blame them? . . . Like in that film 'The Birds'. . . . Human flesh . . . wonder what it tastes like . . . human flesh . . . cannibals, of course . . . do it all the time . . . Fancy an arm, Fred? . . . Nah, I'll have a slice of roast buttock . . .

' 'Morning, Sheaffer.'

'Oh, Henry, I didn't see you there. Good morning.'

'Good holiday?'

'I forget,' said Sheaffer, 'but I think so.'

'You look pale, Sheaffer.'

'Yes,' said Sheaffer. 'I'm not feeling terribly well.'

'Well, take it easy. See you around.'

'Sure,' said Sheaffer, as he pushed open the door of Logan's General Stores. . . . 'Course he will . . . stupid thing to say . . . see you around . . . Everyone does it now . . . like good morning. . . . No one means it . . . Honesty . . . I hope you break your neck . . . I hope your dinner is cold . . . I hope you will both be exceptionally unhappy . . . bad luck then . . . see and do badly . . . don't drop in ever again . . . the meal was simply horrible, Lady Winterbottom . . . your teeth could do with a good clean . . . I say, have you washed yourself lately? . . .

'Excuse me, sir, can I help you?'

'Yes, please,' said Sheaffer. 'Some aspirin, please.'

. . . Bit plain . . . lovely hair, though . . . passable . . . Logan's daughter, I suspect . . .

'There,' said the girl, laying the bottle of aspirin on the

counter as if they were precious stones. 'That's ten pence, please.'

'Thank you,' said Sheaffer, 'and could I possibly have a glass of water to wash them down with?'

'Dad,' shouted the girl through to the back of the shop, 'bring through a glass of water.'

'Wot?'

'A glass of water, Dad.'

... Yes ... Logan's daughter ... definitely ...

'Glass o' bluddy water, God Struth,' said the man.

'I'm very sorry to inconvenience you,' said Sheaffer to the girl.

'That's quite all right, Mr. Sheaffer,' she replied.

'You know my name,' said Sheaffer, who could not recall her unfamiliar face and hoped he had not previously encountered the girl during drunken revels.

The girl nodded.

The man Sheaffer presumed to be Logan brought through the glass of water. 'Who's it fur then?' he asked aggressively.

'Me,' said Sheaffer. 'You see, I'm not feeling terribly well.'

'Neither am I,' said the man, handing Sheaffer the glass and walking back into the rear of the shop with a grunt.

'I saw your photo in the paper last year,' said the girl.

'So that's how you know my name.'

The girl nodded as Sheaffer swallowed the aspirin and the water and screwed up his face in disgust at the taste. 'You make this—don't you?' she squealed suddenly, taking a tube of Sheaffer toothpaste from behind her back and holding it horizontally six inches from Sheaffer's nose.

57

'Well,' said Sheaffer, blinking, 'my employees do.'

'How many have you got?'

'Oh, I can never remember,' said Sheaffer, 'but around a hundred thousand or so scattered throughout the world.'

'*Really!*' said the girl in amazement. 'That must be really wonderful.'

'Why?' asked Sheaffer pointedly.

'Well, I mean,' said the girl, 'running a business and all that.'

'Oh, I don't run anything,' said Sheaffer, looking at the girl as if she should have known better. 'We have people who know about these things to do that. I mean, can you think of anything more boring than running a toothpaste empire?'

'Working in your father's shop,' said the girl.

'Well, I must go. Thanks again. 'Bye,' said Sheaffer.

' 'Bye,' said the girl wistfully.

Sheaffer walked on his way—if more steadily, then not appreciably so. The church bells had stopped ringing. Everyone, he thought, would be singing the first hymn, or beginning the mass, or chewing peppermints, or fumbling to see if they had remembered their money for the offering.

' 'Morning, Sheaffer,' said a small man with a small moustache, who bore himself well, was dressed well, looked very well, and spoke with a smooth and rolling Oxford accent that exuded old-school breeding and indestructible self-confidence.

'Ah, good morning, Professor Swish,' said Sheaffer, and added 'How are you?' in a voice that suggested he hoped the reply would be favourable.

'Oh, well as ever.'

. . . Always the same . . . fit as a feather . . .

'And did you have a productive summer then?' asked

Professor Swish in a voice that suggested that Sheaffer's summer had been most unproductive.

'Exceptionally so, sir,' said Sheaffer, hoping to surprise and deflate. 'I should have the thesis complete by July, and the book by August.'

'Oh, so we're thinking of publication already, are we?' said Professor Swish in a very sarcastic voice.

'Quite so. I've been given the go-ahead, sir,' said Sheaffer, administering the *coup de grâce* and resisting the temptation to laugh aloud. 'The publishers are very keen.'

'Actually, Sheaffer,' said Professor Swish, deciding it was time to change the subject, 'I would like to have a word with you sometime tomorrow—something in mind that I think will interest you.'

'Splendid,' said Sheaffer. 'I'll call in during the afternoon, if that suits you.'

'Indeed, Sheaffer, it does.'

' 'Bye then, sir. Do give my regards to Mrs. Swish.'

'Thank you, Sheaffer.'

Wonderful man, thought Sheaffer, as he sauntered off in the direction of Clarissa's Café. . . . Truly wonderful . . . greatest living authority on sects . . . arrogant . . . pompous . . . cynical . . . pride comes before a fall . . . but not him . . . Onward, sect after sect . . . *Concise History of Sects*, by Oscar Swish . . . my professor . . . my mentor . . . Yes . . . I am his mentorite . . . without whom this book would not be possible . . . *Some Passing Thoughts on Albigensian Atrocities* . . . for my mother . . . by Sheaffer . . . Something wrong . . . Pen name . . . yes . . . Nick Tracy . . . Ed Morgan . . . Gatsby McGraw . . . T. S. Sheaffer . . . D. H. Sheaffer . . . Agatha Sheaffer . . . How about Henry Wadsworth Sheaffer . . . or George Bernard Sheaffer . . . Here's a good one . . . Ralp Waldo Sheaffer . . . Sir Arthur Conan Sheaffer . . .

Better still . . . Percy Bysshe Sheaffer . . . now I like that
. . . Percy Bysshe Sheaffer . . . edited by Sheaffer . . . cover
design by Sheaffer . . . published by Sheaffer . . . and Sons
Limited . . . The Sheaffer Press . . . God, here comes the
rain . . . get soaked . . . *trempé jusqu'à la peau* . . . Mr. Sheaffer has achieved a rare feat . . . Mr. Sheaffer's controver-
sial book . . . in the preface to the nineteenth edition of his
work, Mr. Sheaffer, Regius Professor of Sects at Oxford . . .
in one of his rare interviews said . . . I will never sell the film
rights . . . first and foremost the book was for me . . . Really,
Professor . . . Yes, really . . . *Albigensian Thoughts* to be
published in paperback . . . *Albigensian Thoughts* outsells
Bible . . . *Albigensian Thoughts* translated into Hindustani
. . . *The Percy Bysshe Sheaffer Reader* . . . *The Collected
Works of Percy Bysshe Sheaffer* . . . in twelve volumes . . .
paper or cloth . . . Sheaffer unexpurgated . . . Sheaffer's
greatest hits . . . *Percy Bysshe Sheaffer: The Man and His
Music* . . . the Sheaffer *String Quartet* . . . Wolfgang Ama-
deus Sheaffer . . . Ludwig van Sheaffhoven conducts . . .
'Albigensio' . . . Percy Bysshe Sheaffer at home . . . *How to
Succeed in Sects Without Really Trying* . . . *Mein Kampf*
by Sheaffer . . . today . . . quietly . . . at his home . . . his country home . . . the greatest sectologist of our time . . . Percy
Bysshe Sheaffer . . . loved by all who knew him . . . a man
who did not suffer fools gladly . . . He is great only in parts
but there he is unsurpassed and may never be surpassed . . .
towers among his fellow men . . . always a commoner at
heart . . . shunning a life of toothpaste and denture cream
. . . Her Majesty has sent a message of sympathy to Lady
Sheaffer . . . the Lady Beatrice Sheaffer . . . no flowers . . .
but they came . . . in their thousands . . . roses . . . smiling
in Picardy . . . remember him as he would have wished, said
Lady Beatrice . . . active until the last . . . legend in his own

lifetime . . . this is a sad night for occupational therapy.
. . .

Clarissa's Café was dark and gloomy, almost empty, and those who were there sat silent in newspapers, peeking at pictures. Sheaffer walked into Clarissa's with a cigarette in his hand, wondering whether he should light it or leave it for later, after he had eaten. Then he decided he didn't feel at all like eating anything. He looked at his watch, which registered eleven-thirty.

' 'Morning, Clarissa.'

'And how are you then, lad?' said the plump, red-faced, and red-aproned Clarissa, good-natured as ever, emerging from behind the biscuit display case.

'Great, Clarissa. How's George?' said Sheaffer, smiling.

George was Clarissa's husband; Clarissa had no time for George any more.

'Dreadful,' said Clarissa.

'Is Jack in?'

'Back corner,' said Clarissa. 'Coffee?'

'Black, please,' said Sheaffer, nodding, and deciding after all to light the cigarette. 'Anything new in the jukebox?'

Clarissa shook her head, and her body shook with it; involuntarily; rhythmically. 'I think it's going to rain,' she said.

'It already has,' said Sheaffer, taking his coffee. 'Thanks, Clarissa.' He walked to the back of the café where the Jack after whom he had inquired was seated, reading a newspaper, the front page of which was facing Sheaffer. STARTING TODAY . . . WONDERFUL WORLD WE LIVE IN SERIES . . . E. P. DAWLEY LOOKS AT THE FLAT EARTH SOCIETY . . . ALCOHOLISM, A REASSESSMENT . . . *Our Special Reporter* . . .

' 'Morning, Jack.'

'Sheaffer!'

'Himself.'

'You look pretty rough.'

Sheaffer nodded in complete agreement. 'You know, Jack,' he said, easing himself into a chair with a languid moan, 'you are the only person I know in this whole place who won't ask me what I did for the summer, because you simply don't give a fuck. For that I thank you.'

'You know something, Sheaffer,' Jack replied, laying down his newspaper, 'every bloody person I've met for the past three days has asked me just that. Every bloody person. And you know, Sheaffer, I did nothing—nothing at all—and it was one of the best bloody summers I've ever spent in my life.'

'My father has *never* done anything,' said Sheaffer.

'Well, the thing is,' continued Jack, 'that no one believes you—they just don't bloody believe you. No one believes it's still possible to do nothing any more. Charter flights everywhere—everyone with a car—cheap returns on the bus and the train—everyone trying to get us to do things. Well, I just went home and sat on my arse for three months. I read everything by Tolstoy and Dostoevsky, and, to tell you the truth, I didn't enjoy any of it, but I thought I'd have to read them sometime and it was better to do it then than have to go back to them later. But it was just so bloody great not to have to worry about losing passports or tickets or swimming in dangerous currents, or eating all that horrible foreign food. And I enjoyed it, Sheaffer—more than any other summer, believe me. And as soon as I come back here, they're all on my back. Elsie Gillan—she's the worst. "I went to America," says Elsie. "Have you ever been to America, Jack?" And you know the way she says "Jack", all long and drawling like, as though it was the name for a cream bun that's gone off, or something. "Yes," I said, "I've been there, Elsie; twice, in fact, and it was the biggest pain in the arse of my life." "Oooh, Jack," says Elsie, "I loved it—all the cross-cultural experience." "Cross-cultural experience, Elsie," I said, "is a load of absolute shit. People are the same everywhere. But everyone goes around looking for differences." "Oh, nonsense," says Elsie. "Look at all the materialism." "Materialism, Elsie," I said, "now what's that?" And then she went on in that horrible whiny voice of hers about all the advertisements and the huge supermarkets and the neon lights and all that shit, and I put my arm on her shoulder and I said, "Elsie, has it ever occurred to you that there are more advertisements and shops and neon lights because bloody America is forty times the size of the country you live in yourself?" And you know, it never occurred to the woman. Raving on she was about materialism and cross-cultural differences and the poor creature just didn't realise that it makes no difference where you go, because people are always the same—out for themselves before they give a damn about anyone else.'

'You really are a misanthrope, Jack,' said Sheaffer. 'But I agree with you. What's the article on alcoholism like?'

'Very good,' said Jack. 'Really very good. It confirmed my suspicions. I really am one.'

'An alcoholic?'

'Definitely.'

'So am I,' said Sheaffer, having another sip of coffee.

'Perhaps we should do something about it, Sheaffer?'

'But then we might get completely cured.'

'That's a point,' Jack said morosely.

'My trouble with drink,' said Sheaffer, 'is the same as my trouble with smoking. Most people dislike both intensely when they try them for the first time. I adored my first cigarette, and after my first drink I poured myself an even larger one.'

'I was very ill after my first drink,' said Jack, 'but I haven't been ill since.'

'You mean you threw up?'

'Uh huh.'

'I throw up about once a month,' said Sheaffer. 'I always try to stave it off for as long as possible by breathing fresh air at the window. But sometimes I can't hold it back and it falls all twelve floors to the ground. Fortunately, there are never many people passing at that time of night. It takes seven seconds for it to reach the ground. I timed it once.'

'It's a terrible thing, alcoholism,' said Jack, 'but we just have to live with it.'

'It's not really so terrible,' said Sheaffer. 'Imagine having to work regular hours or something really dreadful like that.'

'No, neither it is.'

'In fact, it's very enjoyable for most of the time.'

'Very,' said Jack. 'You know, Sheaffer, the first time I realised I was an alcoholic was when I saw an advertisement by Alcoholics Anonymous saying: "Can you imagine midterm without a drink?" And I sat down and thought about it and I said to myself, "Jack, can you imagine *any* weekend without a drink?", and then, by natural progression, "Can you imagine any *day* without a drink?" And you know— and it's not that I go out of my way to get it—I just keep finding a glass or a bottle in my hand at the strangest times.'

'Oh, I definitely go out of my way,' said Sheaffer. 'It's as difficult for me to walk past a pub as it is for my father to do anything that requires effort. In fact, when I really have to work hard, I have a special route that takes me to the library whereby I don't pass a single bar on the way.'

'And, of course,' said Jack, 'you can't eat or drink in the library.'

'Or smoke,' said Sheaffer.

'Or kindle flame,' said Jack.

'I wonder what they'd do,' said Sheaffer, 'if someone walked in with a plate of fish and chips, a pint of beer, and some cigarettes, and then started letting off firecrackers at the check-out desk.'

'Throw them out,' said Jack. 'Incidentally, how's the book?'

'I need one more decent atrocity for the last fifty pages, and it's finished.'

'What's the best atrocity?'

'Well, it's a difficult question,' said Sheaffer, 'but the molten lead and carving-knife treatment is my favourite.'

"Tell me about it.'

'Well, Jack,' said Sheaffer, 'finish up your coffee first. You might not feel able to afterwards.'

'It's finished.'

'Ah, good,' said Sheaffer, his face lighting up. 'Then I'll begin.'

2

'Ah, Sheaffer,' said Father Scraw, 'do come in, my boy. Everyone is upstairs. You don't look terribly well, you know.'

'I don't feel terribly well,' said Sheaffer, as his feet sank into the vestibule carpet of All Saints' manse. 'What was the sermon like then, Father?'

'Appalling,' said Father Scraw, 'simply appalling. It was all about arrogance and how we are the slime of the earth and all sinners. He took it from "Let him amongst you who is without sin cast the first stone." '

'Ah yes,' said Sheaffer, 'John eight, verse seven.'

'Oh, I don't know, Sheaffer,' said Father Scraw. 'I was always bottom of the class at Episcopal College; never could remember much about parables except the one about changing the water into wine.'

'Wasn't that just a miracle?' asked Sheaffer.

'Both,' said Father Scraw. 'It was also a lesson to us all that if we want something badly enough we can have it.'

Sheaffer nodded. 'I can't stay,' he said. 'I'm sorry, Father, but I must go back to bed. I can't last much longer on my feet.'

'Oh no,' said Father Scraw, obviously disappointed. 'Got some more Madeira, you know—but I must admit the company isn't up to much.'

'Well, I really am sorry, Father, but I've got some important work to do tonight, and I must sleep first. Can we clear up the matter of the books now? Five minutes should do it.'

'Let's go into the lounge.' They walked through and sat down in soft plush beige armchairs.

'I have a plan, Father,' said Sheaffer.

'A plan?' Father Scraw looked puzzled.

'Yes,' said Sheaffer. 'You need money to repair the steeple. We can get the money—or at least some of it—from selling the books.'

'But, Sheaffer. . . . I mean, some of them are disgusting and . . .'

'I sincerely hope so—the dirtier, the better,' said Sheaffer. 'With pornography, cost is directly proportional to dirt. To put it scientifically, p_1 over d_1 equals p_2 over d_2.'

'Well, it troubles me very much,' said Father Scraw, sounding untroubled.

'Yes—I fully understand that,' said Sheaffer, trying to sound sympathetic and businesslike at the same time, 'but it will also trouble you if the steeple falls down and kills everyone who happens to be underneath. Now, how many books are there in colour?'

'About five dozen.'

'Can you remember any of the titles? This is very important.'

Father Scraw paused and thought for a bit. *'Unfaithful Wives,'* he said. 'There're about twenty of them.'

'Five pounds apiece,' said Sheaffer, smiling and noting it down.

'How about the contraceptives?' asked Father Scraw hopefully.

'They can stay,' said Sheaffer, shaking his head vigorously. 'They are valueless nowadays; everybody uses the pill, except for very stupid people and some Roman Catholics. Try to think of some more titles.'

'*Passion in Paris,*' said Father Scraw tentatively, with a weak smile.

'Oh, you mean *Paris Passions,*' said Sheaffer. 'That's excellent—it's a very recent publication—in colour too, and all pictures. How many of those?'

'About a dozen.'

'Superb,' said Sheaffer. 'They cost at least twenty pounds apiece. How many books are there altogether?'

'About a hundred.'

'Then we can make almost a thousand pounds, and that would be a real boon to the steeple fund.'

'But what if we get caught, Sheaffer? I mean, my position, and . . .'

'Impossible,' said Sheaffer, cutting in, 'utterly and completely impossible. I take the books and give you the money. My contacts in the world of pornography will fix everything. You see, my father was an underground publisher before his first conversion—after which he turned to toothpaste. Two of my uncles still deal in obscenity. They will pay well for Swedish material. Your name will not be mentioned.'

'But they *are* obscene, Sheaffer,' said Father Scraw, 'very obscene, and I am, after all, a churchman.'

'But look, Father,' said Sheaffer, 'the people who read these books are already depraved and corrupted. Looking at dirty books simply prevents them from perpetrating dirty acts. We are doing nothing wrong, Father, believe me.'

'You make it sound like a noble duty, Sheaffer. I am not so sure.'

'The steeple is at stake,' said Sheaffer, who felt that the occasion called for dramatic words. 'These books have been mysteriously placed at our disposal. We must do *something* with them.'

'We could burn them,' said Father Scraw, without a trace of conviction in his voice.

'You don't really mean that, Father,' said Sheaffer.

'No—I don't,' said Father Scraw, bracing himself for the formal renunciation of a position he had never believed in anyway. 'I think that what we are doing is wrong, and possibly even a little wicked—but it is not evil, Sheaffer. Consider the parable of the talents, which suddenly springs to mind—of the man who hid his talent in the earth and was a sluggard—note that well, Sheaffer. To hide these books, whatever their content, would be wrong. We must suppose that they have been given to us for a purpose—in this case the purpose being the repair of the steeple—a worthy cause. And, as you so rightly say, Sheaffer, so very rightly, the steeple may fall down at any minute. And to kill is worse than to corrupt, Sheaffer— and, now that I think on it, what we are doing is not to corrupt but to appease—to appease, Sheaffer, nothing more than to appease.' Father Scraw looked at Sheaffer for his approval. Sheaffer nodded, a very approving nod. 'We will go ahead, Sheaffer.'

'I hoped you would think that way, Father. I think we are doing the right thing.'

'I could do with a drink, Sheaffer. Could you?'

'Perhaps a little daytime nightcap,' said Sheaffer. 'It will help me sleep.'

Father Scraw took a bottle of Chivas Regal from its hiding place within a huge Japanese vase and fetched two crystal glasses, which he filled generously.

'Cheers, Sheaffer,' he said. 'To the steeple.'

'To the steeple, Father.'

'And to our mysterious benefactor,' said Father Scraw.

'You didn't give him your name, did you? They can't trace the books to here?'

'Oh *no*,' said Sheaffer emphatically. 'Payment in cash—no receipt, no names, no nothing.'

'Excellent,' said Father Scraw, 'simply excellent. You have done a good job, my boy.'

'I suppose, in a sense, I have,' said Sheaffer.

3

CARTWRIGHT scooped the skin from the top of his coffee, checked to ensure that he was alone, and popped it into his mouth. He chewed it, swilled it around in some saliva, and gulped it down. As it slid slowly towards his stomach, the smile on Cartwright's lips assumed almost orgasmic proportions. Ever since his childhood the sticky supple taste of coffee skin had held great fascination for him. Few knew of this most innocuous of fetishes; it was a closely guarded secret which had not impeded his worldly progress. At forty-two, Cartwright was the youngest ever to head the Secret Service. Moreover, despite long hours at his desk and the strain that resulted from controlling an international spy network spanning the world, Cartwright was basically a happy man.

As he sat in the Prime Minister's waiting lounge, however, Cartwright was perturbed. He had reached the peak of his profession through a diligence and vigilance that none of his colleagues possessed, but since he had assumed the top post, only one year ago, he had begun to lose his grip. In previous years he had dealt with spies at first hand, but few now visited his richly furnished office at Scotland Yard. Cartwright had, in fact, lost track of several spies in the past few months, not to mention several secret codes; but he had lost track of something much more important than a few common, or garden, spies and codes, and that was why he awaited his audience with the Prime Minister with some concern.

Cartwright contemplated the ceiling. It was a very ordinary ceiling, and Cartwright had expected a much more elaborate affair, with perhaps even the odd fresco. Cartwright had never been to see the Prime Minister before; Cartwright was scared.

The door opened, and a semi-attractive middle-aged woman asked Cartwright to please come with her. Cartwright thought that she looked more like a nurse than a secretary. He rose and moved slowly to the door—rather too slowly, thought the secretary, for one about to meet the Prime Minister for the first time. But Cartwright saw no need to hurry. What man in his right mind does when demotion or instant dismissal faces him? Probably, though, he thought, he would only be pensioned off; or suspended on half-pay; or perhaps they would send him to the Inland Revenue, where there was less scope for failure.

The Prime Minister greeted Cartwright in the hallway. 'Good to see you, Cartwright,' he said.

If only he knew, thought Cartwright.

'Come and take a chair,' said the Prime Minister, leading Cartwright into his study. Cartwright sat down in front of the Prime Minister's desk. It was a comfortable seat, contrasting sharply with Cartwright's frame of mind.

'Now,' said the Prime Minister, 'what's the problem, Cartwright?'

'Well,' said Cartwright, 'it's the antiballistic-missile designs, sir—the Russian ones, sir—a problem has arisen, sir —a considerable problem, sir.'

The Prime Minister felt he ought to look grave. He leaned forward and put both elbows on the desk; deep furrows appeared on his red balding brow.

'Exactly how considerable, Cartwright?' he asked.

'I've lost them, sir.'

'God,' said the Prime Minister. 'You haven't!'

'Yes, sir,' said Cartwright, 'I have.'

'But . . . I mean . . . well,' spluttered the Prime Minister disbelievingly, 'you just can't have lost them, Cartwright, you just cannot.'

'I assure you, sir, I have lost them.'

The Prime Minister said nothing, but closed his eyes in anguish; he opened them again and glared at Cartwright with an icy coolness, tempered with an unwillingness to absorb what he had just heard.

'Are they in the country, Cartwright?' he asked.

'I hope so, sir.'

'Whatdoyoumean?' roared the Prime Minister. 'The head of my own Secret Service telling me he *hopes* the most important secrets we've had in years are where they damned well ought to be!'

Cartwright gave the Prime Minister a couple of seconds to cool off and continued. 'They arrived on Friday, sir, on the SS *Asparagus*. My agent arrived at the dock an hour later, and they had vanished, sir. Vanished.'

'And you have no clues, Cartwright, no clues at all as to where they have vanished to?'

'Only one, sir,' said Cartwright, who felt he should be shaking but was now completely numbed by his destiny. 'But it's so slim as to be almost worthless. The warehouseman sold some altar wine to a young man about twenty minutes before my agent arrived. Now the microfilm was stored in cases almost identical to those of the altar wine, and was, in fact, lying alongside the wine cases. The young man may have been given the cases accidentally, or, of course, he might have appropriated them when the warehouseman was fetching his change—that is, *if* he was an enemy agent.'

'What on earth,' said the Prime Minister, 'was microfilm doing in cases as big as that?'

'Concealed, sir,' said Cartwright, 'concealed in the packages. The films were sent through Finland and Sweden and then shipped to London. The Russian agents in Sweden are particularly sharp, sir, we so . . . well, sir, what we did was . . . we photocopied the microfilm of the designs on to . . . well, on to condoms, sir.'

The Prime Minister's mouth fell open. 'Are you really asking me to believe that, Cartwright?' he said, his voice trembling; on his lips, a watery smile.

'It has been used before, sir,' maintained Cartwright. 'The great Nitzikovich used it; condoms are mentioned in the transcript of his trial—*Nitzikovich* versus *The United States*—in 1954.'

'Oh, God,' said the Prime Minister, scratching his chin. 'This is dreadful—awful, almost. The waste of time, of money, of men. And if it gets out, the opposition will kill us. Besides, apart from everything else, it also puts the country in great danger, which is bad for the party's image. Surely you have something to give you a lead?'

'Unfortunately not,' said Cartwright. 'The warehouseman did not remember much about the young man. All I know is that he was of medium build, well spoken, wore dark glasses, a soft hat, and a white raincoat.'

'Oh dear,' said the Prime Minister, 'spies do tend to dress like that, don't they?'

'Only in films, sir,' said Cartwright.

'And you have no more information on this man?'

'He could have been anything from eighteen to thirty, sir. He said very little to the warehouseman. All he said was that he had a sore head and he was going on a long journey.

He also said something about sex, sir, but the warehouse-man didn't catch all of it.'

'What about sex?'

'He said that he studied it, sir.'

'How disgusting,' said the Prime Minister.

'Anyway,' said Cartwright, 'that's absolutely all we have, sir. He paid cash and left no name.'

'What was the make of his car?' asked the Prime Minister.

'No one we spoke to saw it, sir.'

'Sounds like an expert to me, Cartwright,' said the Prime Minister. 'And, of course, no prizes for guessing where his long journey was to—back to Russia, of course.'

'Hardened spies don't usually tell people they are going on long journeys, sir.'

'You may not think so, Cartwright,' said the Prime Minister, pursing his lips, 'but to me this man sounds like a professional espionage agent with perhaps sexually maniacal tendencies. But whether he is, or whether he's just an overgrown choirboy with a dirty mind, you had better find him, Cartwright, or you will find yourself working for the Inland Revenue.'

'I'll do my best, sir,' said Cartwright unconvincingly, 'but it may take some time.'

'You have three days, Cartwright.'

'But, sir . . .'

'Seventy-two hours, Cartwright, to find this fellow and those condoms.'

'Thank you, sir.'

'Miss Kelly will show you out, Cartwright.'

Miss Kelly took Cartwright to the door and returned to the Prime Minister's study.

'You know, Miss Kelly,' said the Prime Minister, 'it's not really much fun being prime minister.'

'Really, sir,' said Miss Kelly, smiling understandingly and mentally noting his remark for her memoirs.

'I think I shall speak to the nation tonight,' said the Prime Minister. 'Call the BBC, Miss Kelly, and tell them . . . tell them I want fifteen minutes around nine o'clock.'

'What will you speak on, sir?' asked Miss Kelly.

'What was it last time?'

'The economy, sir.'

'Oh, Lord,' said the Prime Minister, 'that's so incredibly boring. I think I shall speak on our role in the world today.'

'They won't like it, sir,' advised Miss Kelly.

'Who? The BBC?'

'The nation, sir,' said Miss Kelly. 'You see, "Star Trek" is on at nine, and if you requisition the time, the BBC will have to cancel it.'

'Can't have that, then,' said the Prime Minister. 'I want to watch it myself—never miss an episode. Then I think I shall play my harmonica for a while. I can speak to the nation tomorrow.'

4

THE interior of All Saints Episcopal Church displayed the
sort of tasteless extravagance one expects to find in the home
of a wealthy parvenu. Gaudily painted statuettes of saints
in blue, red, and flaking gold decked the pillars of the aisles
and the small alcoves of the transepts; the more popular
among them flickered in the light of an obsequious candle.
In the nave and chancel, the Virgin herself in various ages,
colours, poses, and sizes overlooked the congregation with
an expression dependent on the mood of her sculptor. Sometimes she stood rigidly with Saint Joseph, looking as if she
had come to accept life as a tolerable succession of tragedies
organised by God and therefore, *per se*, worth while. Sometimes she stood demurely beside Saint Anne with a goat or
a lamb, and even the odd cherub, and at other times she
smiled down on her son as tenderly as any mother would
on an infant who never cried or wet his bed or woke up
everyone in the manger at four in the morning.

On the walls of the aisles, the fourteen stations of the
cross were inexpertly depicted in variegated greens, browns,
and reds. When blood appeared, even during the scourging,
it was sparingly shed and bright pink in colour. Most of the
figures showed little emotion, although at one station an
oval tear was painted just below Mary Magdalene's left eye.
Jesus himself looked fairly indifferent to the proceedings.

The altar was a prodigious affair, coated with fine green

77

velvet and topped with a dozen or more silver candlesticks. At the back was a plain ivory cross, mounted on teak, while on the wall behind was a larger cross of wood with a golden Jesus pinioned to it. The sides of the altar were lined with highly polished brass vases of slightly wilting roses, and on the ledge before the pulpit were two more vases, with rather fresher flowers.

In the pulpit, Father Scraw half listened to the closing hymn of the evening's service. The congregation was small and quite unenthusiastic, although he did notice one girl of about twenty sitting near the front in a neatly fitting pale green pinafore looking rapt; he had never seen the girl before. The organ droned 'Amen' out of key; hymnals snapped shut; someone sneezed; seventeen backsides clumped on to wooden pews with a dull sense of finality. Father Scraw blessed them all.

'And now,' he said, 'a few intimations.'

Mitchell, the fishmonger, a server for some years, was to marry Agnes, the organist's daughter. Vandals had broken into the Sunday school and desecrated the walls with ungodly words and libidinous sketches. The penultimate announcement concerned the steeple, which, Father Scraw said, was in need of considerable repair. One could not have a church, he said, without a steeple. It was like having a bath without water, or a television set without a picture. The two had what he called a symbiotic relationship. And besides, if the steeple did fall down, it would probably kill lots of people. It was things like that, said Father Scraw, that got Christianity a bad name. And so, great endeavours must be made by everyone. Masons and steeplejacks with any Christian leanings, even if they had been baptised and no more, should be encouraged to lend a hand. Builders should offer free cement, sand, and scaffolding. And all

78

members of the church should give generously to keep God's house in order. 'God's house,' he repeated.

Father Scraw looked down at the congregation and saw fewer guilty faces than he had hoped. The new girl at the front looked a little unhappy; he would chat with her afterwards and make her feel better.

'And now,' he said sonorously, 'I have one further announcement.'

The congregation, he felt, was impatiently silent.

'I have been here now,' he began, 'for thirty-five years. It has been a long time.'

An old man in the front grunted and nodded in agreement. The old ladies pricked up their ears; the girl coughed.

'And,' continued Father Scraw, with practised humility, 'I have never felt I have done all that I might have done here.'

The old man nodded once more. The old ladies leaned forward in their pews. What was it? Resignation, retirement, defrocking?

'And so,' Father Scraw continued slowly, enjoying himself immeasurably, 'it may come as a great surprise to all of you to learn, as I did this afternoon . . .' He paused; not a sound was heard. 'To learn,' he resumed, 'that I have been made the new *bishop*.'

Sixteen people gasped; the girl smiled. Father Scraw bowed, ever so slightly. The organist struck up the opening bars of 'Zadok the priest' and then forgot what came afterwards. The congregation trickled out, gossiping, and the neatly dressed girl made her way slowly to the door. Father Scraw walked briskly up to her.

'You're new here, aren't you?' he said. 'Come for some tea.'

Mrs. Scraw was at her mother's. They sat down in the

lounge of the manse. Father Scraw put on the kettle and asked the girl her name.

Beatrice told him, and about the job in the hospital, and . . . She paused.

'Yes?' asked Father Scraw expectantly.

'Well . . .' She paused again. 'I work in a bar two nights a week. . . .'

'Excellent,' remarked Father Scraw.

'Should I call you "your Grace"?' Beatrice asked.

'Oh no—not yet, anyway—although some people will, I suppose. What pub do you work in, Beatrice?'

'With Mrs. Wilcox—the Roaring Donkey.'

'Wonderful place,' said Father Scraw. 'Sheaffer goes there. You must know him.'

'Really quite well,' replied Beatrice untruthfully. 'Do you know him too?'

'Backbone of the church—used to take the Sunday school —still organises the fête, the jumble sale, and the steeple fund. Great friend of mine, Sheaffer.'

Beatrice smiled and crossed her legs.

'And he brings the altar wine,' said Father Scraw, beaming, 'every time he comes from London. Incidentally, how is Mrs. Wilcox?'

'Cheerful,' said Beatrice, a little more loudly as Father Scraw fetched the tea and some treacle scones from the kitchen, 'but she misses Harold terribly.'

'Really tragic,' said Father Scraw, buttering a scone. 'I just looked across at him and . . .'

'But I thought . . .'

'Ah yes,' said Father Scraw, 'you won't have heard I was there—nor should you tell anyone. You see, if everyone knew I played dominoes every Saturday night with Sheaffer and Harold Wilcox and Ernie Green in a bar, I might be asked to resign or something. Why—it's a tricky business, the priesthood, Beatrice. Good grief—even when I drop into the Crown for a pint I have to wear a false beard and speak with a Lancashire accent.'

'Everyone speaks well of Harold,' said Beatrice, trying not to spill a chunk of strawberry jam on the carpet. 'I'd like to have met him.'

'Well,' said Father Scraw, 'he had a really bad temper, old Harold, but actually he was one of the best. Tell me, are you going to join the church, Beatrice?'

'Yes,' she replied, without hesitation, as if it were more a matter of blind faith than evangelical calling. 'I'm going to come every Sunday. Perhaps I could help with something.'

'You could always help Sheaffer with the steeple fund.'

'Oh good—I'd love to.'

He liked the way she spoke. Sensing a girlish infatuation in her voice, he instinctively transformed it into something stronger. Never having loved, he looked eagerly for love in those he knew, as if to reassure himself of its existence.

'You can tell him yourself,' he said, smiling and lighting a pipe of rich dark honeydew. Beatrice sipped her tea and said that she would.

Monday

I

CARTWRIGHT considered the Scotch bottle; its neat symmetrical dimples, and the label of embossed gold paper. He thought of the Scottish highland glens it was said to have come from, of the heather, the moss, and the swift streams of clear fresh water cascading. He contemplated what the contents of the bottle had been, and, somewhat ruefully, what they were now. He decided that he had been very foolish; but then, he thought, what would life be, without a reasonable amount of foolishness from time to time.

Cartwright sank back into his comfortable chair and peered at the pink telephone on his walnut desk. Cartwright was very fond of his pink telephone; the only trouble was that it did not ring very often when Cartwright wanted it to; Cartwright hoped that the pink telephone would ring very soon; but then, when he thought about it, he decided there would not be many people around even in London at four o'clock on a wet Monday morning, with any overwhelming urge to telephone him. Cartwright considered the lilies of the field, and wished he could be a lily himself for a while; not forever, though—just for a few blissful mindless moments of serenity; lilies didn't worry about the telephone not ringing; lilies didn't worry, full stop; lucky lilies, thought Cartwright; not toiling, not spinning, not doing anything, in fact; just growing around, winking at other lilies, and getting together with the bees to have baby lillies. Cartwright smiled—and wondered why. He didn't really have much to smile about; but then, so often euphoria springs from that sense of irremediable hoplessness and the knowledge that however dreadful a predicament may seem, it cannot possibly become any worse; that, at least, was how the situation seemed to Cartwright.

Cartwright sighed, reached for the pink telephone, and raised it clumsily to his ear; he pressed extension 1, and, as he did so, his fingernail cracked painfully.

'Fuck,' said Cartwright.

'Ooooh!' gasped the disapproving receptionist.

'Get me a car and a driver at once,' Cartwright snapped.

'At once, sir,' the receptionist replied.

'I want a car with no police signs on it and a nondescript-looking driver,' he added.

'Wilkinson, sir?' asked the receptionist.

'Wilkinson will be ideal,' said Cartwright. He replaced the receiver firmly and deliberately. Enough drinking, he thought, enough sitting around waiting for the telephone and depending on others. The stale dry air of the office had congested his nostrils with stiff slices of snot. He threw open the window, breathed the fresh wet morning air, and drank in the grey mist. Then he put on his checked coat, buttoned it up, and fitted his hat neatly on the top of his head. He walked down to the garage, where Wilkinson awaited him in a 1967 Cortina.

'Tilbury Docks—second gate,' said Cartwright.

Wilkinson swept the car off into the early-morning streets. It was too much to expect the sun to rise; dawn came like a thick grey brush stroke on the skyline of a black city. Cartwright looked at the darkened shops, dim and empty, the ghostly lit supermarkets and food-filled shelves; the glassy-wet pavements.

'Dead, sir,' said Wilkinson.

'Less dead than you think,' said Cartwright.

'One last try, sir?'

'The last,' said Cartwright.

'The men have been over it with a fine-toothed comb, sir.'

'Fuck them,' said Cartwright. 'I'm worth fifty of those idiots.'

Wilkinson thought it best to shut up.

'Easy does it,' said Cartwright as they drew near the docks. 'Second on the left and you're there.'

'Sir,' muttered Wilkinson instinctively.

Two slightly rusted iron gates blocked the way. A drowsy uniformed gateman was aroused and uttered something indecipherable as they approached. Wilkinson reached for his identification.

'No,' said Cartwright quickly, 'leave it.'

The gateman slouched towards the car, dragging his boots in the thick oozing mud of truck wheel tracks.

'Can't come through, guv',' said the gateman apologetically.

'Regulations?' asked Cartwright.

'Special loading traffic this morning,' said the gateman.

'Every day?'

'Depends.'

'What about last Friday?' asked Cartwright.

'Can't remember, guv',' replied the gateman.

'Try very hard,' said Cartwright in an almost hypnotic voice.

The gateman scratched his head and contorted his wizened face.

'Closed all day,' he said.

'You on duty?' Cartwright asked. The gateman nodded.

'You turned someone away that morning,' said Cartwright, taking a five-pound note from his pocket and handing it to the gateman. 'He was about twenty or so, with dark glasses, a white raincoat, and a hat. What kind of car was he driving?'

'Jesus, guv',' said the gateman, 'I turns 'em away by the dozen.'

'Around ten o'clock he came,' repeated Cartwright, lighting a cigarette and handing one to the gateman. 'Think hard. White coat—dark glasses—soft hat—medium build.'

'Exactly,' added Wilkinson, feeling he ought to contribute something, however useless, to the conversation.

'Wot's it 'bout anyway?' said the gateman, who was puzzled, but still quite calm and unconcerned by his remunerative interrogation.

'A hideous murder,' lied Cartwright, rolling the syllables across his tongue to make the invented crime sound doubly hideous.

'Jesus,' said the gateman. 'Don't recall nothin' much, Friday.'

'Ten o'clock,' repeated Cartwright more loudly, for the benefit of the old man's hearing. 'He was coming for something heavy—when you turned him away he probably swore or gave you the "V"'s or something.'

'Ye-es,' said the gateman, painfully slowly. Then he raised his voice in recollection. 'I remember him—said somethin' 'bout red tape an' the like—swore too, the little bastard—dark glasses, as well—you're right there—don't remember no hat, though.'

'What make of car?' asked Cartwright, smiling with cautious optimism.

'Mercedes,' said the gateman. 'Mercedes 600.'

'Good man,' said Cartwright, a little more excitedly than

he had wished to sound before Wilkinson. 'Good man. You don't remember anything else, I suppose?'

'The number, of course,' replied the gateman. 'A *requisitioned* number. Couldn't forget it, even suppose the bloody devil himself was at the wheel.'

'Jesus!' exclaimed Cartwright.

'S-H-2,' spelled out the gateman, in a slow steady monotone.

'S-H-2,' repeated Cartwright, incredulously.

'S-H-2,' muttered Wilkinson, dumbfounded.

'That's right,' said the old gateman, 'S-H-2—don't see many of those cars around here—must be rich or something—bloody foul mouth on the fucking bastard, though.'

'Thank you very much indeed,' said Cartwright as the gateman stuffed the five-pound note into his pocket. 'Thank you again, my friend.'

'Hope you find the whore,' said the gateman.

'Oh, I shall find him,' said Cartwright, smiling superciliously and winding up the window. 'And what's more, Wilkinson,' he continued as the car pulled away, 'I shall find him *myself*.'

2

ANDREW MACKENZIE, a failed turf accountant, had been serving the Royal Mail in the borough of Lindenlee for the past thirty years, and in that time he had lost many letters, stuffed innumerable Christmas cards down drains, and had once even brought about a divorce suit when he had delivered a letter to a woman-in-the-house-next-door. Andrew had, accordingly, no reputation for conscientiousness; nor did he harbour delusions, like many men of his sort, that at the bottom of it all he was really quite a fine fellow. Andrew knew that, at heart, he was really rather a wicked and thoughtless person, but he also knew that whatever he might wish to do with the letter currently gripped in his hand, it was a Special Delivery, and Special Delivery meant just that. Special Deliveries simply couldn't be stuffed down drains or accidentally blown into litter bins; Special Deliveries must be delivered, which, he decided, was a great pity, since there did not seem to be anyone awake to receive this one.

'Mr. Sheaffer,' he called harshly, for the fourth time, as he paced the carpet outside Sheaffer's flat in Manor House, 'Mr. Sheaffer, are ye up yet?' Not being familiar with Sheaffer's life style, Andrew did not appreciate the foolishness of this question. Yet as he put his inquisitive ear to the door he sensed within a faint stirring, and his spirits rose as the stirrings were superseded by gurgles and groans, and eventually by several harshly pronounced words with which Andrew himself was most familiar. This was followed by a few muffled and unsteady footsteps and some blurred oaths.

'Special Delivery,' barked Andrew.

'Yes,' came a drowsy and decidedly irritated response. A hand appeared around the edge of the door.

'Mr. Sheaffer?'

'Himself,' Sheaffer replied, his head emerging around the door like that of a cautious tortoise waking from hibernation.

'Sign here,' said Andrew, handing Sheaffer a pen and a nondescript-looking slip of paper. Sheaffer signed the slip of paper without reading it; then he accepted the letter and returned indoors, rubbing his eyes with the knuckles of his thumbs. Two Alka-Seltzers later he felt a little better; mouthwash too, he thought . . . Mr. Sheaffer, you may be a great sectologist, but in the mornings you have bad breath. . . . Not any more, mate, now that I use Stinko mouthwash . . . keeps my breath foul and nasty . . . The telephone rang. . . . Beatrice . . . can't make it tonight . . . Grandmother eaten by a crocodile . . . in Bury St. Edmunds . . .

'Hello, is that Angela Gray?'

'No,' said Sheaffer. He guided the receiver back into its cradle and peered at the Special Delivery on his desk. . . . Who sends Special Deliveries? . . . People who want something specially delivered . . . kings . . . queens . . . prime ministers . . . Dear Shcaffer . . . time of emergency . . . get country back on its feet . . . man for the job . . . student of life . . . great sectologist . . . one among few . . . yours faithfully . . . the Queen.

'Milk,' said a voice loudly at the door.

Sheaffer opened it. 'Hello,' he said. 'You must be a milkwoman. I've never had a milkwoman before.'

'You're not going to have one now,' said the woman, who looked very agricultural. 'How many do you want a day?'

'One,' said Sheaffer, and closed the door. . . . Never any peace . . . in the mornings . . . one after the other . . .

He returned to his vigil over the Special Delivery . . . Go on . . . open it . . . who could it be? . . . God no . . . police . . . receiving stolen goods . . . SECIOLOGIST STOLE DIRTY BOOKS . . . shame . . . disgrace . . . hanged by the neck until you are dead . . . buried on unsanctified ground . . . SHEAFFER TOOTHPASTE IS DIRTY TOOTHPASTE . . . destitution . . . fall of the house of Sheaffer . . .

He ripped open the envelope, insofar as one can rip open anything at eight o'clock in the morning. He knew at once it was not as bad as he had feared and he began to read it slowly to himself.

Dear Sheaffer,

For many years now I have not been doing anything and finally it has become rather a bore. And so your mother and I have decided to take a long holiday in Antarctica, which we have always wanted to visit. Assuming we don't have many whale or iceberg problems we should be back in about five years.

Now, as you know, son, I have never taken much interest in the toothpaste industry I began, which is now the biggest in the world. All I do is chair the monthly meetings, during which I invariably fall asleep. My reasons for this are twofold. Firstly, I have never, since my days in publishing, believed in exertion of any nature. Secondly, I realised a long time ago that toothpaste, like television sets and pickled onions, is a human necessity, and even if it tasted like sago pudding, people would still buy it rather than go to the dentist more often.

Accordingly, I do not want to ask any great favour of you, but I would like you to take my place in the board room each month and watch over our thriving empire. Should you feel your loyalty to sects is such that you cannot spare the time, I will give the job to Uncle Charles, but I am sure you understand my desire to keep control within the immediate family. Of course, should you wish to be active in the firm (which God forbid), you are free to do so, and you may make any policy decisions you wish, although frankly there is not much policy-making in toothpaste—you just keep churning out the stuff and make sure there are enough toothbrushes around to hold it.

I should say here, son, that something else has been worrying your mother and me lately—namely, the fact that you have now been in the University for eight years. Now, we know full well that you are making broad avenues for yourself in sectology, but we feel in the pits of our being that life in Lindenlee is taken a little too seriously and that you should enjoy yourself more. Each time you write to us you tell us how hard you are working; this worries your mother terribly, and often makes me wonder just where I could have gone wrong in bringing you up. I realise that you did not see as much of me as you might have done in your youth because of the amount of time I spent in bed, or bars, or basking in deck chairs, but I still think that your industrious nature tends to savour of ingratitude. Do try to drink a little occasionally, or go to parties. Relax, lad, that's the keynote to life; not to do nothing, but to do nothing *well*.

I shall say more of this to you *tonight* when your mother and I drop into Lindenlee to say farewell before departing on the whaler *Atlanta* for the Southern Ice Pack. Do book us into a good hotel with an all-night licence, room service, and a late breakfast. Don't bother about getting anything in for your mother and me, except, of course, for liberal quantities of gin, to which, as you know, I am very partial,

Your loving father,
Ernest

. . . God . . . tonight . . . Beatrice . . . Mother . . . Father . . . Something, he decided, would have to be done. . . . Beatrice, I'm afraid . . . Beatrice darling, I meant to tell you . . . It's like this, Beatrice . . . This will not be easy, Beatrice . . . No reflection on you . . . always been fond of occupational therapists . . . 4 . . . 8 . . . 5 . . . 7 . . . bzzz . . . dnk . . . 'Mrs Wilcox?'

'Sheaffer!'

'Mrs. Wilcox, I have a big favour to ask of you. You may have anything in return.'

If only I could, thought Mrs. Wilcox, but I'm too old for that sort of thing now.

'What's the problem, lad?'

'Ask Beatrice to work tonight, and don't tell her I told you. Tell her all the staff are sick or something. You see, I have a date with her, and now my parents are coming. You know what they're like. If they meet her, they'll start saying embarrassing things about getting married, and when's the happy day—you know. And you know how horny my father is?'

'True,' said Mrs. Wilcox, whose bottom had once been pinched by Ernest Sheaffer.

'Well, they'll just put Beatrice right off me,' said Sheaffer, secretly believing that nothing could put any woman off him but not prepared to take the risk this time.

'I'll try,' said Mrs. Wilcox, 'but it won't be easy. She's really taken to you, that Beatrice—or so I think, and I don't want to play the hard mistress.'

'Please—for me—just this once.'

'For you—anything,' said Mrs. Wilcox, clenching her dentures. Then she walked back into the kitchen and finished her fourth bacon sandwich of the morning.

3

' 'MORNING, sir,' said Miss Frome, in her deep husky voice, as her hips swayed like a metronome across to Commissioner Cartwright's desk.

' 'Morning, Lucy,' said Cartwright, stretching his arms as his secretary's almost diminutive but perfectly proportioned form slid into his lap.

'You've got him, then,' said Miss Frome, stroking his cheek with one hand and the trousered rod of his rising penis with the other.

'Guess so,' said a very tired Cartwright. 'I'll know for sure in a few minutes.'

'Mmmmmmh,' responded Miss Frome, running her tongue slowly across her upper lip as Cartwright drew invisible lines with his injured fingernail on the surface of her well-filled blouse.

Cartwright felt Miss Frome's rounded breasts swelling beneath his finger tip as if about to burst out and engulf the palm of his hand.

'Can we—Carty?' she asked, breathing more deeply and gripping his penis like a wall bar in a gymnasium. Cartwright wanted to—very much. He glanced at the long wide couch beside the window, and the almost-firm yellow velvet cushion upon it that reminded him of ravioli and other things. But business was business; he tried to think of thoughts unsexual.

'Business is business, dear,' he said, nibbling her cheek.

'Ooooh, Carty,' she whimpered, as though she had expected his reply but was still disappointed. 'Can't we really?'

'Tomorrow perhaps—if I can sort this mess out,' said Cartwright. 'But meanwhile I must ensure our continued working relationship. Now—be a good girl and send in Veronica with the dossier—the sooner I get this bloody thing wound up, the sooner we can . . . well . . . get back to . . .'

'Bed,' interjected Miss Frome, moving her lower lip seductively.

'Oh, go, Lucy, go, for God's sake,' said Cartwright, 'or I shall have an embarrassing erection for the rest of the day. I'm far too busy to get all worked up.'

'All right, darling,' said Miss Frome, kissing his forehead and giving his penis a parting squeeze. 'I'll send in Virginal Veronica.'

Virginal Veronica strutted officiously into the office with a ten-year-old hair style and black nylons with unattractive seams on not unshapely legs. Nothing wrong with her, thought Cartwright, that a beauty salon and a few good screws wouldn't fix; still, he wasn't going to administer the treatment.

'Sit down, Veronica,' said Cartwright, 'and spill the beans. What's his name?'

'Sheaffer, sir.'

'Sheaffer!' repeated Cartwright, trying to remove a particle of tobacco ash from his left eye.

'As in toothpaste, sir,' said Veronica.

'First name?' asked Cartwright.

'He doesn't have one, sir.'

'Rubbish,' said Cartwright. 'Everybody has a first name. Even the son of God had one.'

'His is just Sheaffer, sir.'

'Where does he live?'

'That depends, sir,' said Veronica. 'He has a cottage in southern France and an apartment in Lindenlee, Scotland, where he spends half the year, sir. His parents live in London, and his father is Ernest Sheaffer, the industrialist. Together they own Sheaffer Toothpaste.'

'That explains the requisitioned number plate, anyway,' said Cartwright. 'Where is he *now*, this fellow?'

'Lindenlee, sir,' replied Veronica. 'You know, sir—the provincial university, sir—it's been on the go for years. He's writing a book, sir.'

'Good God,' said Cartwright, beginning to wake up a little. 'Lindenlee—that's where old Tiger Wilcox died so mysteriously last year with a glass in his hand. One of our best bloody agents too, one of the best ever. We think he was on to something at the time, so he might have been bumped off. Dreadful business—old Tiger Wilcox was one of the best spies this country has ever known—awful tragedy. This fellow Sheaffer—b'Jesus—he might have had something to do with that too.'

Virginal Veronica nodded intently.

'In that case,' said Cartwright, in his most businesslike voice, 'there may be much more to this than meets the eye. Pack my special case, Veronica, with three hundred pounds in cash and my Luger. I'm going on holiday to Lindenlee for a few days. Miss Frome will be accompanying me.' Cartwright reached for the telephone and pressed the extension button, with greater care this time. 'Get me the Prime Minister as soon as you can,' he said. He replaced the receiver and turned once more to Veronica.

'Anything else, sir?' she asked.

'One more thing,' said Cartwright. 'Contact our agent up

there—the chap we sent to replace Wilcox. Tell him I shall be arriving tonight.'

'It was a woman we sent, sir.'

'Oh, of course, Veronica,' said Cartwright, chuckling. 'Imagine my forgetting that. Lovely little thing she is too— wouldn't believe it to look at her that she could shoot a man dead at fifty yards.' His memory paused. 'What was her name again, Veronica?'

'We call her Amanda, sir,' Veronica replied.

4

'I'M looking for Jack,' said Sheaffer to the young lady at the Dental Hospital reception desk. 'I've known him for years, but I'm afraid I don't know his second name.'

'Huh,' mumbled the receptionist. 'We have thousands of Jacks here. What does he look like?'

'Medium build,' said Sheaffer, 'with a friendly sort of face. I don't think he does very well in his examinations, if that helps any.'

'You must mean Jack Bendex then,' said the receptionist, as if she had just found Livingstone in darkest Africa.

'Probably,' said Sheaffer, looking at his watch, which showed nine-thirty. 'Where can I find him at this ungodly hour?'

'At his chair in the surgery, of course,' said the receptionist coyly. 'All the students work on patients in the morning.'

'Thank you—I have a very important message to give him.'

'No one,' said the receptionist severely, 'is allowed into the surgery except the patients.'

'I know,' said Sheaffer, preparing to be very untruthful, 'but—it's his mother. She's been ill for years, and . . . well . . . actually we expected it, but I thought if I broke it gently . . .'

'God, no!'

'God, yes,' replied Sheaffer. 'You understand, an errand of mercy.' He passed into the treatment room.

Sheaffer had never been in a dental hospital before; in fact, he had never gone to a dentist's at all until unbearable pain forced it upon him; consequently he strode with some trepidation down past the long rows of dreaded chairs with the drills hovering like the hand of death above each suspecting patient. A wandering dental superintendent, imagining correctly that Sheaffer had no right to be there, approached him like an angry head nurse.

'Jack Bendex,' said Sheaffer, trying hard to smile. 'I'm looking for him. In fact, I have an appointment with him,' he added, his capacity for telling lies being augmented the more embroiled he became with the experiment.

'Over there,' said the superintendent, without indicating any direction. Sheaffer made for the far corner of the treatment room, suffering the sound of grinding drills and the suppressed screams of the patients. . . . God . . . hell on earth . . . cauldrons full of fillings . . . How many did you pull today, mate? . . . Only ten . . . poor show . . . much blood . . . couple of gallons . . .

'I'm looking for Jack Bendex,' said Sheaffer to a fresh-faced young man who looked much too nice to be a dentist. 'Do you know where he is?'

'Over there,' said the fresh-faced dentist, wielding his needle timidly.

'Thank you,' Sheaffer replied, speeding his pace to avoid witnessing the patient being injected.

Jack was busy when Sheaffer arrived, although he looked much too drowsy to be busy at anything. His patient seemed to be undergoing severe nervous strain.

'It won't hurt,' said Jack diffidently, 'really.'

Five seconds later the tooth was in the disposal bucket.

'See,' said Jack, feeling enormously satisfied with himself, 'it didn't hurt at all now, did it?'

'Never knew it was out,' said the gratified patient, putting on his coat.

'Sheaffer—good to see you,' said Jack, turning abruptly. 'Never knew you were next on my list.'

'Well, actually, Jack, I'm not, and I just came to . . .'

'Take a seat anyway—and I'll give you a quick check-up.'

'You promise you won't touch me at all?'

' 'Course not,' said Jack as Sheaffer got into the seat. 'Unless there's something wrong.'

'Now look here!'

'Open wide,' said Jack. 'Dear, dear, dear. How much do you smoke a day?'

'You know damned well how much I smoke.'

'Obviously a great deal,' said Jack, who despite a copious alcoholic intake had never smoked a cigarette in his life and secretly resented all smokers. 'Your tongue is disgusting.'

'Positively disgusting,' repeated a passing instructor. 'Do something about it, Bendex. NO, wait a minute. This is good experience for the others. Come on, you chaps,' he added, raising his voice. 'Gather round and see what a disgusting tongue this chap has.' Before Sheaffer could do anything, the instructor had gripped his tongue and had almost ripped it from the back of his throat.

'Disgusting, isn't it?' he said aloud.

'Positively mossy,' said a seedy-looking student.

Sheaffer did not know what to feel; he just felt generally awful.

'This is what happens,' said the instructor to the small white-coated crowd that had gathered round to observe

Sheaffer's tongue, 'to someone who smokes too much. What should be done about it, Bendex?'

'He should brush it, sir,' said Jack.

'You mean actually *brush* it?' doubted an insecure-looking student, who didn't seem to have eaten anything for some years.

'Of course,' said the dental instructor with overwhelming arrogance. 'You can brush your tongue like your teeth. This fellow,' he said, pointing to Sheaffer, 'should brush his tongue three times a day.' Then the instructor clapped his hands loudly.

'Back to your chairs,' he ordered, 'and get on with the business of filling and extracting. But remember well: Brush a mossy tongue, and it will be mossy no more. And now,' he added, turning to Jack once more, 'brush it, Bendex—and brush it well.'

Jack prepared a special brush which dentists sometimes employ on people whose tongues are in a similar state of deterioration to Sheaffer's.

'While you're at it,' continued the dental instructor, taking a greater interest in Sheaffer's toothwork, 'fill that cavity in the rear molar. And *don't* close your mouth,' he commanded as Sheaffer tried unsuccessfully to avoid further indignities.

'Wider please, Sheaffer,' requested Jack, who was now determined to do a good job in front of the instructor. 'This should be quite tricky, sir,' he said.

'Tricky?' said the instructor contemptuously. 'Nothing tricky about it, Bendex—except that it's so filthy I doubt if you could clean it properly if you used sulphuric acid.'

Sheaffer felt very small and exceptionally unhygienic. He decided, in the brief calm before the treatment began, that his days had been loosely spent and his evenings passed in

extravagant dilatoriness. Now even one of his best friends
had revealed him for what he was: an unworthy and un-
cleanly sectologist. All his initial anger departed from him
like a fishing smack leaving a stormy sea for a becalmed
harbour. He decided that he had discovered himself and that,
all things considered, he was not charmed with his discovery. He closed his eyes, considered prayer, but could
not think of anything suitably appropriate to say to the
Almighty.

Five minutes later his tongue had been successfully
scrubbed, and rinsed in a fluid that looked like plaster of
Paris and tasted rather like the smell of camphor.

'Good job, Bendex,' said the instructor. 'Now fill the
tooth.'

Sheaffer, having rinsed, was told to open his mouth wide.
The needle was unsheathed; it seemed to glisten in the bright
white light and hang in his mouth for minutes before sliding
deeper and deeper into the gum. Although he had expected
pain, he still found it a bit of a shock having his expectations
fulfilled; strange, he thought, in a stoical moment, how rarely
that happens with pleasant expectations. The drilling of
the tooth seemed to last an age, principally because Jack
had not been a dentist for long and did not want to make a
mistake in front of the instructor.

'Rinse now, mate,' he said when he had finally hitched
the drill back on its hook, 'and we'll be through in a jiffy.'

Sheaffer rinsed once more with the fizzy pink fluid. The
filling was mixed by a young nurse who reminded Sheaffer
of a reindeer. Then Jack proceeded to squirt the filling into
his tooth with a special instrument for squirting fillings into
teeth. Sheaffer enjoyed that part; when the drilling was over
he always felt safe; after all, they were putting stuff in, not
taking it out.

'Thank you, Gladys,' said Jack when the filling was safely locked in the tooth, 'you can go now.'

Gladys went, tripping daintily across the green-tiled floor. In the chair to Sheaffer's left, a young boy was telling his mother that he didn't need her to hold his hand. Sheaffer thought he looked the well-behaved type who would wash behind his ears without being told to. He decided that the boy's courage suggested strongly he had never seen or heard of a dentist before in his life.

'Well,' said Jack, removing the napkin from around Sheaffer's neck, 'wasn't so bad now, was it?'

'For a time I was annoyed,' said Sheaffer, truthfully. 'In fact, during the tongue incident I was decidedly embarrassed, and I hate to think of what will happen if news of it gets out to some of the girls I am accustomed to kissing. As for the filling, I needed it; courage simply failed me, until it was thrust unavoidably in my path. But needless to say, I came here on more important business.'

'Come for some coffee,' said Jack. 'We have a break now. I suppose it's something about the Scraw incident you want to see me about.'

'The very same,' said Sheaffer, 'but it has to be done to-night.'

'I'm free tonight.'

'To go to London?'

'Oh yes,' said Jack, ducking to avoid the outswung arm of a drill. 'I have an uncle in prison there. I can visit him when I've finished the job. And I can visit my mother—she has flu.'

They passed by the reception desk on their way to the coffee room.

'Mr. Bendex,' said the receptionist with meticulously feigned grief, 'I'm so sorry to hear about your mother.'

'Oh, don't worry,' said Jack cheerfully. 'Very soon she'll be up and doing the same things she always was.'

I wish I had his faith in the hereafter, thought the receptionist as they walked away.

5

Susan Elliot's mother was making treacle scones in the Georgian Hotel when her daughter came to call. Professor Herbert Ramsbottom, Mrs. Elliot's latest lover, was sitting on the sofa, unshaven and in his dressing gown, eating thickly buttered slices of well-done toast.

' 'Morning, Suzie,' said Mrs. Elliot as her daughter, in a bright-red trouser-suit, skipped through the door. She turned to her Rupert of the Rhine. 'You really ought to get dressed, Herbie,' she said.

'Yes, Herbie,' said Suzie, giggling, 'Rupert of the Rhine always shaved before eleven in the morning.'

'He had a beard,' said Herbie, dryly and unmoved, being now accustomed to his colloquial nomenclature in the Elliot household. 'Have you finished that essay for me yet on the execution of Charles I, Suzie?'

'Tomorrow, perhaps,' said Suzie. 'But it's so terribly difficult, Herbie. I just don't know why you can't give me an easy one to do for a change.'

'Now, Suzie,' said Mrs. Elliot, 'don't go expecting favours from dear Herbie just because we've taken him into the fold, as it were. That's dishonest.'

'Oh, it's all right,' said Herbie, secretly thinking it was all wrong. 'I'll give you an easier one next time.'

'Now isn't that nice of Herbie?' said Mrs. Elliot. 'Suzie, dear, put these scones in the oven while I fetch Mr. Phifer's breakfast. Mr. Phifer is from the United States, dear—he's staying here for a week or so.'

There was a knock on the kitchen door, which then opened to reveal a portly gentleman in his late fifties whose appearance strongly suggested that he originated from the New World. He wore a tartan tie, an outsized kilt, and carried a thick edition of the poems of Robert Burns under his arm.

'Hi,' said the portly gentleman, 'my name is Phifer. I thought I'd show you my kilt. Gee, Mrs. Elliot, is that your daughter?'

'No,' said Mrs. Elliot, forgetting that Mr. Phifer was cross-eyed, 'that's Professor Ramsbottom. My daughter is beside the oven.'

'Hi,' said Suzie. 'How do you like Lindenlee?'

'Just fantastic,' said Mr. Phifer with great gusto as he moved from side to side to demonstrate the expensive pleating of his kilt to the best advantage. 'As for this man Burns,' he added, holding the book with loving affection against his tartan tie, 'I don't exactly know what he's saying, but I really dig the way he says it.'

'Professor Ramsbottom is a Stuart historian,' said Mrs. Elliot. 'He writes books. You may have heard of him?'

'Can't say I have,' said Mr. Phifer.

'No harm done,' said Herbie. 'I haven't heard of you, either.'

'Have you ever been to Loch Lomond, Mr. Phifer?' asked Suzie. 'It's really lovely.'

Mr. Phifer smiled and gave up wondering whether the last remark Herbie had made was pleasant, unpleasant, or neither. 'No, darn it,' he said, letting off a low rattling fart. 'But I saw Ben Nevis on Thursday and I just can't wait to tell the folks back . . .'

'Yes,' interjected Mrs. Elliot, who was afraid Herbie

might insult Mr. Phifer in a way he might understand. 'But, of course, you have your Grand Canyon and your Red Indians and your peanut butter, which we *don't* have. So you're just as well off as we are.'

'Gee, Mrs. Elliot, it's mighty nice of you to say so,' Mr. Phifer drawled.

'Well, come and eat your breakfast,' said Mrs. Elliot, 'or it won't be fit for human consumption.' She carried the tray into the dining room, and Mr. Phifer strutted behind her like a pregnant turkey, whistling the tune of 'Bonnie Dundee'.

'I wonder if he's just a bad example to them,' said Herbie. 'I mean, they can't all be like that or they'd still be sailing around in the *Mayflower* looking for land.'

Suzie put the scones in the oven as Mrs. Elliot returned with an empty tray.

'Isn't he sweet?' said Mrs. Elliot.

'Very,' said Suzie. 'By the way, Mother, I met Sheaffer a few minutes ago. He's decided to have a farewell party for his parents in the Roaring Donkey tonight, after closing time. They're going to Antarctica. We're all invited.'

'How lovely,' said Mrs. Elliot, who had once been on a ski trip with Ernest Sheaffer before he had met Mrs. Sheaffer.

'Is that the toothpaste Sheaffer?' said Herbie. 'That lunatic's father?'

'Sheaffer is no lunatic,' said Suzie angrily, 'and you watch what you say about him in this house. Thanks to Sheaffer's knowledge of East London bars, Mother was able to trace father's address and begin divorce proceedings against him.'

'Sorry,' said Herbie, who wasn't.

'And you remember, Herbie,' added Mrs. Elliot, in her schoolmistressy voice, 'you be on your best behaviour with Ernest Sheaffer and with his wife. That woman is deeply religious, and if you use any disgusting words in front of her, she'll hit the roof. Remember that, Herbie, remember that well.'

Herbie gave up. Ten essays to mark, a lecture to prepare, an insatiable woman to satisfy, with a daughter who thought that Marco Polo was the capital of China. He went to the bathroom, to wash, perchance to shave. Women, he thought, as he soaped his scrotum, women!

6

THE doctor's waiting room was crowded, but everyone had arrived after Sheaffer except for one girl, whom the doctor had been treating for the previous half hour. Sheaffer had been there for forty minutes now, musing on God, buttered parsnips, and recent trends in brewing. Morning light filtered into the waiting room in splinters, and within the splinters Sheaffer could see all the minute particles of dust in the air he was breathing; still, it seemed to taste all right; he decided that if it had been detrimental to health, someone would have done something about it long ago, so he made up his mind not to bring it up as a new subject matter with the old lady beside him, with whom he had been conducting a desultory conversation for the previous ten minutes. His mind turned to other matters.

. . . Beatrice . . . what if she refuses to work? . . . He's my sectologist and you can't take him away from me . . . and he loves me . . . so he does . . . or do I . . . What if she died? . . . The Lady Beatrice, my Lord, is dead. . . . She should have died hereafter. . . . She was a woman, Horatio, in whom I had an absolute trust . . . fair . . . like fields of barley . . . sweet as a succulent plum . . . with a great big dimple on her cheek . . . and another on her bum . . . infatuation . . . Mother, I love her. . . . Nonsense, boy, you're infatuated. . . . Hence, Le Sheaffer Infatué . . . Mother, I'm going to marry an occupational therapist. . . . No occupational therapist will ever set foot in this house. . . .

'My sister is an occupational therapist,' said Sheaffer, once more striking up the desultory conversation with the old woman.

'Really,' said the woman, trying to sound interested; she pursed her lips; wrinkles cut sharply from her nose to her mouth like the map of the delta of a great river.

'You *do* know what that means,' said Sheaffer.

'No,' said the old woman.

'Well, it's a person who massages other people,' said Sheaffer, trying to mime a physiotherapist at work. 'It's really a sort of commercialised yoga.'

'That's foreign, isn't it?' said the old woman with a hint of distaste in her voice that suggested mild xenophobia.

'Very,' said Sheaffer. 'The Indians practise it extensively, as do the people of southern Turkestan. They have big public displays of massaging there. In fact, the southern Turkestan motto is "You massage my back and I'll massage yours." '

'Have you ever been there?' inquired the old woman.

'Only once,' said Sheaffer, 'but I'll never go back. You see, massaging is really a very ethnic thing. It's never really caught on in Britain except among golfers and football players, who, of course, require extensive massaging after every performance.' With this remark Sheaffer smiled and the conversation closed yet again. He decided that whether Beatrice was going to work or not that night, she just couldn't meet his parents except in passing. Hints and obscene suggestions by his father had, after all, lost him the beautiful Lady Gwendoline, the Maid of Drumkinnes. He must never make the same mistake again. It would do no harm to introduce them to Beatrice at the party as a good friend, but as a date—that was different. It implied suggestions of affection between the two, which would start both Mother and Father off in their very different yet equally damaging ways. It would be a testing evening, whatever happened.

Sheaffer's name was suddenly announced over a crackly speaker above the door. He walked briskly up to Dr. Bean's office just as the girl who had gone in more than half an hour before came out looking much happier than before she had gone in.

'Do come in, Mr. Sheaffer,' said Dr. Bean.

'Thank you, Doctor,' said Sheaffer, smiling benignly. Dr. Bean seemed to twitch continually; his hands were spread before him on the desk and shook violently, almost as if he was driving an armoured car over rocky terrain. Sheaffer noticed he had no fingernails; for a brief moment he considered asking the doctor what *he* could do for *him*, and then he decided it might appear to be rather rude.

'I shouldn't smoke,' said Dr. Bean, 'but do you mind?'

Sheaffer said, 'Certainly not,' and took out his own pipe.

'You have a problem?' the doctor asked, burning his fingers with a match and dropping both the match and the partially lit cigarette on to the floral carpet.

Sheaffer retrieved Dr. Bean's cigarette, lit it, then lit his own pipe.

'The problem,' repeated Dr. Bean, twitching in rhythm and scratching his nose, 'what is it, old boy?'

'Well,' said Sheaffer noncommittally, 'it's rather difficult to explain.'

'You can tell me anything,' said Dr. Bean, extending his arms in a 'people-of-the-world-unite' gesture.

'Well, it's a sexual problem.'

Dr. Bean breathed deeply, and his face lit up like a nova. 'Good,' he said. 'I mean, bad. What I mean is, I can help you, I think.' He went to the cupboard by the door and took out several files, all of which seemed to be concerned with sexual ailments. 'I am a bit of an expert at this,' he added as he returned to his chair.

'It's really quite embarrassing,' said Sheaffer, looking a little sorry for himself.

'Nonsense,' Dr. Bean remarked leisurely. He had stopped twitching now and seemed more at ease. 'Now what exactly is it that you do that worries you?'

'That's the trouble,' said Sheaffer disconsolately, 'I don't do anything. You see, I've lost interest.'

At this Dr. Bean broke into spasms of throaty laughter and spluttered all over a sheaf of important-looking papers. Then his face fell and his voice sounded much more official and serious than before. 'Dear me,' he said, 'you mean you . . .'

'Yes,' said Sheaffer, 'I just don't care any more.'

'You don't think you're becoming a . . . well, you know?'

'Certainly not,' Sheaffer replied. 'I am still as fond of women as I always have been. I've just lost the urge to . . .'

'I don't like asking this—but you haven't had gonorrhoea?'

'Under no circumstances.'

'And so,' continued Dr. Bean, 'you won't have had the other one, either?'

Sheaffer looked perplexed and shook his head.

'Syphilis,' said Dr. Bean, as if it was the dirtiest word in the English language. 'You know, the thing Delius died of.'

'I don't think you quite understand, Doctor,' said Sheaffer. 'I have never been a particularly concupiscent person, although there were times when my wild oats were spread more thickly and universally than they have been of late. Not that I wish to revert to this position. But I would like to regain some of my initial stimulus for sexual adventure.'

'Indeed, indeed, indeed,' said Dr. Bean with complete empathy. 'This is what we must aim for in the long term. But it will not be easy, Mr. Sheaffer. You must try to reintegrate yourself with the sexual process. Tell me, does this do anything to you?' he blurted, whipping out a colour photograph of a naked model strewn across a bed of unusually dry autumn leaves.

'Nothing at all,' said Sheaffer, 'but then, how can you expect it to when the real thing leaves me absolutely cold?'

'True,' said Dr. Bean, 'but I had to ascertain the extent of the problem. Many men delude themselves that they don't want sex simply because of its unavailability.'

'You mean because they can't get it.'

'Or cannot perform,' added Dr. Bean, rolling his r's with relish.

'No problem,' said Sheaffer, confidently but unexcitedly. 'I have no shortage of female friends; in fact, one of them is a . . .'

'Sex maniac,' interrupted Dr. Bean. 'Is that it?'

'Well—yes.'

'Then that's it,' said Dr. Bean jubilantly, throwing his arms in the air and spraying saliva over the desk, the carpet, and Sheaffer. 'You are rebelling against a morbid desire in a female friend for sexual satiation.'

'You mean that because she likes it, I don't?'

'Frankly—yes.'

'Well, what do I do about it?'

'You take one of these tablets after breakfast every day,' said Dr. Bean, producing a small transparent box of tiny green tablets. 'These are medicinal aphrodisiacs called "sexules". In the business we say: A sexule a day drives the frigid away. They were invented by a man called Ramupsavich, a naturalised Persian of Russian extraction who had

difficulty in adapting to harem life after years of mono-
gamy.'

'And will this cure me?' asked Sheaffer hopefully, slip-
ping his pipe into his pocket.

'In time—yes,' said Dr. Bean, 'but do remember that
practice makes perfect. If you take the tablets and during
the course of the next few weeks you fail to revert to your
torrid days of old, then you may build up great cravings for
women whose enthusiasm is not equal to your own. And
that could lead to problems.'

'I'll handle the situation with discretion,' said Sheaffer,
'but you do promise they work?'

'In a shot,' said Dr. Bean, 'hahahaha. Not only do they
give you desire again, but they also help you to . . . well . . .
get your water pipe to harden at the critical moment.'

'Well, thanks again, Doctor,' said Sheaffer, rising and
making for the door.

'You'll keep me in touch with your progress now, won't
you?'

'Certainly,' said Sheaffer, clasping the tablets in his hand
and moving slowly backwards on the way out.

Dr. Bean leaned towards his microphone to summon the
next patient from the waiting room. 'Mrs. Grimbles.'

A chair scraped on the waiting-room floor and an extra-
ordinarily obese bus conductress with breasts the size of
five-pound bags of sugar trundled in the direction of the
surgery door.

' 'Bye,' said Sheaffer, clutching his sexules protectively.

'Good shooting,' said Dr. Bean, laughing lasciviously.

The bus conductress belched loudly and thundered into
the office.

Sheaffer glided out into the street; a light wind creased
his hair and whipped his tie over his shoulder. A celery

sandwich for lunch, he decided, with some H.P. sauce, then a pint of black creamed Guinness with a monstrous head on it. Then a little nap, a visit to Professor Swish, and a few odds and ends before the moonlight flitting of the books from Father Scraw's. Life was wonderful, he thought; well, perhaps not so wonderful; perhaps it was even awful, but it was never so bad when you thought you were better than everyone else, and were.

'Watch out,' screamed a passing motorist, jamming on his brakes.

'Sorry,' said Sheaffer apologetically. 'So sorry,' and added, 'My mind was elsewhere.'

7

TEA break in the hospital. Beatrice was thinking about the recent past.

From her seat in the train she had seen the dry Solway moors slide by, the slabs of sliced peat, and the redstone houses with their strong foundations, bleak by the roadside. Then the haul to London, sleepy in the late afternoon with the cigarette smell and the half-finished coffee stale in the plastic cups, stickying the tables heaped with crisps bags, folded and rolled in balls or rustling on the floor of the fast train.

Then London, weary, like she was, with night falling, the warm hotel that they had paid for, with room service and proper maids; and even a drink in bed, brandy it was, at midnight, with ginger, dry. Then the long deep sleep of the night, with no nerves and not even a visit to the toilet; a pity, she had thought, since she had one all to herself, and a bath, which she took in the morning as the daily paper slipped under the door at seven; seven, and the postman scarcely out and about; she heard the milkman move below, saw the traffic lights bright in the narrow streets and the yellow headlights of the cars, strangely silent from the high window of her room; dawn reluctant to show, yet so beautiful, she thought, with just a suggestion of it.

Bacon for breakfast, three rashers, Ayrshire, crisp, well done, she said, as people said of steak sometimes. She had an egg too, soft and easy to dip into, with fresh bread and patted butter. Then there were the pavements, crowded, and the building she came to, tall and new and exciting; modern, she thought; and the office with the lush carpet, the semi-circular desk of polished mahogany, and the most expensive waste-paper basket she had ever seen in her life. He was friendly, almost familiar. She accepted a cigarette; menthol. He had a cigar. Did she have doubts? None at all. She really thought it was just for her. Did she have the patience? Yes. She knew she could do it.

He thought she could do it too. He liked her green pinafore; he said so; and her aquiline nose; although he didn't say that; perhaps he though it was too big; still, it hadn't mattered. Congratulations, he said, I hope you're with us for a long time. She hoped so too. Thank you, she said.

Now she sat in the coffee room in the hospital and sipped her tea. A fly settled on the arm of the dusty sofa. She read the telegram on her lap once more: ARRIVING TONIGHT. CROWN HOTEL. URGENT BUSINESS. CARTWRIGHT.

Dear me, she thought, I wonder if I really can do it, after all.

8

IN London it was almost time for lunch. At 10 Downing Street the Prime Minister was playing 'The Blue Danube' on his harmonica and getting the bits in between the choruses all wrong. Pausing for a smoke and a pink Plymouth, he began to prepare for lunch with a Middle Eastern dignitary. He took out his Arabic phrase book and repeated the words for 'perhaps' and 'we shall see' several times. Glancing at the Arabic for 'Why don't we get to know each other better?' he remembered Cartwright and shook his head slowly in despair. After lunch, he thought, he would earmark an eminently boring place for him in the hierarchy of the Inland Revenue.

'Miss Kelly,' he called to his secretary, 'bring me in a salted cucumber for Ivor. He's very hungry.'

Miss Kelly came in and tossed the salted cucumber to the Prime Minister's pet monkey on its perch.

'Now, eat that and shut up, Ivor,' said the Prime Minister scoldingly. 'Daddy has some words to learn for lunch.' He unwrapped a caramel and chewed it with suppressed delight, hoping that nothing particularly eventful would happen in the world that afternoon; if not, then the first spot on the national news would be his for the third day in succession.

Meanwhile, in Eaton Square, Ernest Sheaffer was munch-

ing pork chops and reading the September number of
Leisurely Pursuits.

'Hargreaves,' he called to his valet, 'is Madame back yet
with my stock of cigars for Antarctica?'

'Not yet, sir,' replied Hargreaves, emerging from the kitchen clad in a thick furry overcoat and a furry hat.

'Really, Hargreaves!' said Ernest Sheaffer, 'I know you
are intrigued by the new outfit we bought you for the Antarctic, but do remember we still have to cross the equator
and the tropics before we reach our destination. I meant to
ask you—are you sure you do want to come? We may be
gone six years, you know.'

'Well, sir, there is just one problem.'

'If it's peppermint creams, Hargreaves, don't worry—
I've arranged for a six-year supply to meet your luggage
at the dock.'

'Actually, it's my wife, sir. We are rather close, sir,
and . . .'

'Well—bring her along with us, man, for God's sake,'
said Mr. Sheaffer with his customary panache. 'She'll be
good company for you on the long Antarctic nights. You
do know about the long Antarctic nights, Hargreaves? The
sun simply never rises, and if you go out walking in the
dark you can run into walruses and penguins and God knows
what else.'

'The missus would be happy to accept your offer, sir,'
said Hargreaves, trembling with emotion and boundless
gratitude.

'Good show,' said Ernest Sheaffer, finishing off the chops
and discarding the remainder of the apple sauce. 'Good
meal, Hargreaves. Now, I have something rather important
to tell you. Will you have a seat?'

'Thank you, sir.'

'No—not there, Hargreaves—sit opposite me at the table. Have some wine,' he added, pouring a glass of claret for his valet. 'It's about Communism,' he said, with some conviction.

'God forbid, sir.'

'Nonsense,' said Ernest Sheaffer, stroking his beard lovingly. 'Now that I have decided not to become a Roman Catholic, I feel I need something to replace it with. From now on, I shall be a Communist, and my household will be run on Communist principles. Obviously, of course, I shall still not do any work, but nevertheless we are all of us equals from this day forth. You and Mrs. Hargreaves will eat at the same table as Mrs. Sheaffer and myself on our journey to, and during our stay in, Antarctica. On no account will you call me "sir" or my wife "madame". We will become Ernie and Ethel—you and your wife will become Frank and Myrtle. Is that understood, Frank?'

'Sir.'

'Ernie to you.'

'Yes, Ernie.'

'Thank you, Frank. Now clear the table if you will and take off that ridiculous coat and hat. Our plane leaves for Scotland in two hours. There is much to be done.'

This said, Ernest Sheaffer rose from the table, went into the bedroom, and snatched a quick forty winks before his regular afternoon bath.

Meanwhile, at Heathrow airport, Cartwright was laughing at a thriller in which the detective got his man. Damp mist hung above the runways; flights were delayed by almost an hour.

'Get yourself a drink,' he said to Lucy. 'In fact, get me one too.'

She rose obediently and walked to the bar with the rounded shoulders of a weary waitress about to go off duty. Why did he treat all his women so badly, he wondered—yet they all seemed to obey him as they would obey an ailing father. Even his two wives would have swept the Augean stables spotless and still have had his dinner on the table at seven. Perhaps he was just a good lover—no, he was more than good. Dozens of women and a knack of learning lessons from all his affairs had built up within him a formidable body of carnal knowledge. Even from his less successful lovers he had gleaned data that had helped him in later encounters; he was a good gleaner, he knew that. In sexual matters, he thought, was the ultimate proof of the theory that one learns most from one's mistakes. It is repeating the successes that is most difficult. But then, success had still strayed in his wayward path as often as wild deer meander on to country lanes. He laughed to himself, thought briefly that he should feel slightly ashamed, and was neither pleased nor disturbed that the capacity to do so eluded him.

Lucy returned with the drinks, and he put down the thriller.

'You do have a gun, dear?' he asked, raising his glass to his lips.

She nodded.

'Good,' said Cartwright with determination. 'You may need it tonight. It's as easy for the upper classes to get guns in this country as it is for the working classes in America.'

'You really think he's dangerous?'

'We take no chances,' said Cartwright, feeling enormously important. 'Our country is at stake.'

And so it bloody was, he thought fleetingly. How ironic that condoms, which had, until the invention of the pill, served him so faithfully, should now carry the makings of his undoing. Justice, he feared, might be done; or was it really justice? Unfortunately, it was; positively poetic, in fact. Still, it would make a damned good story when he sold his memoirs to the Sunday papers.

'Our flight,' said Lucy suddenly, 'it's just been announced.'

'Good,' said Cartwright, 'good, good, good.' Tired though he was, he rose abruptly; there was life in the old lecher yet, he thought. Visions of the Inland Revenue began to fade. He wasn't going to write his memoirs for a long time. With luck, by the end of the day he would have another chapter; and a chapter of successes at that.

9

IT was crisp in Lindenlee; twelve-thirty, and not much shopping going on; stores closing for lunch, cafés busy, pubs quiet, churches empty. In the Georgian Hotel, Susan Elliot was making Mr. Phifer's bed, while her mother manicured her toenails and listened to 'Farm Special' because she was too lazy to turn the radio off. In Clarissa's Café, Jack Bendex was wolfing down a heaped plate of toad-in-the-hole, the only food he ever had for lunch except at Christmas, when he ate turkey to please his parents. Down the road in the Roaring Donkey, Sheaffer was eating a celery sandwich and explaining to a travelling salesman the fundamental textual problems faced by the modern sectologist. On the other side of the bar, Mrs. Wilcox crammed meat pies into a small oven and picked her nose nimbly with alternate movements of her left hand. And in All Saints Episcopal Church, Father Scraw was carving a candle into some sort of shape, and humming 'In the Bleak Mid Winter', his favourite carol, which he caused to be sung by the congregation once a fortnight, winter, spring, summer, and autumn.

Father Scraw was in a particularly good mood that morning. Brisk sunny weather, combined with the news of his long-awaited promotion, filled him with an extra special goodwill. Sitting, as he was, in the front pew, with an old newspaper unfolded at his feet to catch the candle shavings, he felt that had he not answered the call to the church forty years before, life might have destined him for breath-taking exploits of adventure. And, as he hummed, he fancied he was a polar pioneer, fashioning a weapon to kill the day's provender with. Perhaps he should have gone to Africa, tramped through the jungles, and brought the gospel to the natives. Dr. Scraw, I presume. Still, he might not have been very good at that, since he hated forcing things down people's throats, especially if they didn't speak English. He worked best with the converted—he knew that. Persuasiveness had never been one of his talents, even when it came to persuading himself; he was good at reassuring other people, though, even if he didn't agree with them at all.

Australia, now, that would have suited him. Plenty of sheep, Alice Springs, the Great Barrier Reef, and Botany Bay, where all the convicts went. He thought that if chance had made him a convict, he might have rather enjoyed Botany Bay; swimming and sunshine and plenty of mutton, a game of cricket in the afternoon with a kangaroo as wicket keeper, and a bit of waltzing with Matilda at night. Better than dancing with his wife, anyway. Still, he loved her in the sense that she was stable and predictable and because she always knew the right thing to do even if he preferred to do something else. He could invariably foresee when she would disagree with him, and he invariably decided ahead of time when he would give way and when he would fight to the death for his own point of view. Never having lost his temper since a cricket match in his teens, he knew he held a guillotine blade above her head; she would always be afraid he might lose it again. For Father Scraw, then, politics was entirely domestic. He had never voted in an election in his life and always abstained at church synods, principally because he never understood any of the issues being discussed.

Perhaps that was why they had made him a bishop—no one could possibly hold anything against him. Yet in no sense did Father Scraw feel more than mildly irresponsible, except when he tipped the sherry bottle a little too far. He believed implicitly that he lived life the way God would want him to lead it. Everyone was irrational—even Christ had accepted the ointment rather than give it to the poor. Wine was in and sin was out; but what was sin anyway? He wasn't terribly sure; but God knew, and Father Scraw felt a great common bond with God. Father Scraw suspected that, in between listening to prayers and performing miracles, God enjoyed a quiet drink, a good joke, and an occasional pipe of rich dark honeydew after meals. After all, what else was there in life, terrestrial or everlasting? Sex was out—he was far too old for that now. Jesus had never given it much thought. God was certainly past it. Such was life. Indulge in the pleasures of your age and don't worry about fate. Predestination. It was all worked out anyway. He thought it had worked out pretty well for him.

Father Scraw laid the candle on the newspaper and wrapped the pieces into a tight ball. He hadn't made anything with it after all. Still, that was the fun of carving a candle; you just never knew what exciting creation you might come up with. In years to come, men might gaze in awe and say, 'Scraw made that', or, 'Here is a classic example of Scraw in his later period'. This time, however, Scraw hadn't made anything at all. He trudged to the vestry, threw the newspaper into the waste-paper basket, and sighed happily. He took his false beard from the bottom drawer of his desk, fitted it neatly to his chin, and set out in the direction of the Roaring Donkey.

IO

'She said she had an engagement with someone special,' said Sheaffer to Mrs. Wilcox for the seventh time. 'I suppose that must mean *me*. Pity about that, but I must admit I'm flattered. Someone special, eh? I suppose I really must be.'

'Listen to him, for God's sake,' said Mrs. Wilcox with affected exasperation as she resumed the foraging of her right nostril. 'Ah!' she exclaimed, pleased. 'Some more customers.'

Into the lounge of the Roaring Donkey walked two girls, one looking as if she had gone to a Swiss finishing school, the other as if she wished she had. Behind them came a cautious Father Scraw, replete with false beard and looking rather like the man who stands around in station toilets collecting the money if you decide to wash your hands and face. Father Scraw, in his bearded form, was known to his friends as Albert.

' 'Morning, Albert,' said Mrs. Wilcox cheerily. 'The usual?'

'Mackeson, please, Miriam dear,' he replied in his adopted Lancashire accent, which would have done any Bolton man credit. 'Sure, but I've 'ad a 'ard day down the pits.' Then he remembered there was no coal mines within a radius of twenty miles, so he shut up quickly and hoped the two girls were not spies from the Ecclesiastical Synod. He heaved an internal sigh when they continued unbuttoning their coats without looking up. Perhaps, he thought, they didn't know where the nearest pit was, either.

Mrs. Wilcox handed Father Scraw a frothy Mackeson.

'There we are, Albert,' she said. 'Lovely day, isn't it?' she added, raising her voice and directing her last remark to the two girls. One of them smiled. The other tried hard, but just failed; her lips sank like an inverted fan, revealing good teeth, slightly yellowed, inefficiently cleaned. The first girl carried a translucent blue umbrella, which she put down, after some hesitation, by the door. Perhaps, thought Sheaffer, she had heard about Scottish pubs in her Swiss finishing school.

The girl who smiled was obviously the spokesman for the two. 'Could we have two lemonade shandies, please?' she asked.

'Pint or half-pint, dears?' asked Mrs. Wilcox cheerily, unaware of the fact that girls who go, or wish to go, to Swiss finishing schools never drink pints of anything, even milk.

'Half-pints, please,' said the spokesman.

'Good to be up in the air again,' said Father Scraw, forgetting, once more, the local absence of coal mines.

'Are you a miner?' asked the spokesman, sounding interested, and surprised, because she had always imagined miners to be covered with black dust, even at home.

'He used to be,' interjected Sheaffer, who knew what a bad liar Father Scraw was. 'And he still thinks he is, in fact. Isn't that right, Albert?'

Father Scraw nodded aggressively, and Mrs. Wilcox passed over the lemonade shandies.

'You see,' said Sheaffer, continuing his exegesis, 'Old Albert caught the bends, a disease common to deep-sea divers and coal miners, which makes you think you're still down there although you're not. Isn't that right, Albert?'

'Right on,' said Father Scraw, forgetting he was supposed to come from Lancashire and using his American Negro voice.

'This is lovely shandy,' said the girl who hadn't said a word before.

'You're very kind,' said Mrs. Wilcox, moved, as are all women when someone congratulates them on doing a job usually performed by men.

Father Scraw remembered his beard was false and stopped tugging at it.

'Where are you headed?' Sheaffer asked the girl who had just spoken.

'We're going to Aberdeen,' said the girl, 'but we're hoping to spend the night with someone here. You don't know of anyone called Sheaffer, do you?'

Mrs. Wilcox's face lit up, and her mouth poised on a syllable. Sheaffer stared her into silence.

'How awful,' he said. 'How strange and how sad. What was his other name?'

'He didn't have one,' said the spokesman, confused by Sheaffer's last remarks. 'It was just Sheaffer.'

'Then it's the same one,' said Sheaffer, shaking his head and running his hand ruefully down his left cheek. Memories of ribald times in Geneva drifted back. But why didn't they recognise him?

'How well did you know him?'

'Oh, he's a great friend of our brother, Angus Hardy. Look—exactly what's going on?'

. . . Good old Angus Hardy . . . best billiards player in the Western Hemisphere . . .

'He's dead,' said Sheaffer. 'I'm sorry, this will come as a great shock to you and to Angus—your brother Angus. He died last week.'

Both girls gasped loudly, and the spokesman said, 'Oh no!'

'Multiple sclerosis, it was,' said Sheaffer, thinking it was a convincing enough name for a disease that you would expect someone to die from. 'It was very sudden. He felt no pain. I knew him well. Happy until the last.'

'How terrible,' said the girls in unison.

'We all miss him,' said Sheaffer.

'Used to work in the pit,' said Father Scraw, trying hard to sound inane and succeeding to a creditable extent.

'Yes, yes, Albert,' said Sheaffer, and, turning to the girls, 'I know, too, that he would have loved to meet you. He often spoke to me about your brother and what a fine billiards player he was.'

'Oh, how true,' said the spokesman. 'How nice of him to remember.'

'He was more than nice,' said Sheaffer. 'He was a very great sectologist; had he lived, he would have been knighted, or something of that order.'

'Well,' said the spokesman, trying to look suitably sad for the occasion, 'that's how it goes.' She drained her glass.

'We must be off,' she said. 'Angus *will* be sorry to hear the news.'

'He probably knows,' said Sheaffer. 'Telegrams were sent to the nearest and dearest. I received one myself. I shall always treasure it.'

Sheaffer helped the girls with their coats while Father Scraw ordered another round of drinks and mumbled something about Davy lamps. But just then the bar door opened, and Jack Bendex sauntered jovially in.

'Hi, Sheaffer,' he said.

Mrs. Wilcox rubbed iodine into the deep gash the translucent blue umbrella had gouged on the top of Sheaffer's head, while Father Scraw and Jack held his arms to prevent him from resisting the necessary treatment. The two girls were gone, and only the faint odour of expensive perfume remained, sifting into Sheaffer's nostrils while he shrieked, gurgled, and kecked several times as the stinging iodine soaked into his skull. Never again would he tell lies. He had lost a good friend in Angus Hardy.

Still, what could he have possibly done? The date with Beatrice was unavoidable now, and, in any case, exciting, promising much; besides which, his parents would be here in a few hours. Girls from Swiss finishing schools were de lightful in Switzerland, but Lindenlee presented its own unique problems. He could leave Switzerland at two hours' notice; Lindenlee he had to live with, at least until his sectual masterpiece was complete.

Sheaffer's kecking and moaning having subsided, Mrs. Wilcox's deputies released their hold on his arms. 'Look after the bar, Jack, if you would,' she said, 'and serve anyone who comes in. I'm going upstairs to do some ironing.' Jack said that he would. No lunchtimes were every busy in the Roaring Donkey, Mondays particularly.

They sat down by the electric fire opposite the door. 'Serious news,' said Sheaffer seriously, nursing his head. 'The books must go tonight. I called my uncle yesterday evening with lists of titles, and he can use them all. But he must have them for distribution tomorrow. Fashion in pornography changes even more quickly than fashion in clothes.

Conceptions of the libidinous modulate with frightening speed. Unclothed one day, semiclothed the next. Cartoons are coming in, in a big way, and Swedish orgies are so common now, there is no scarcity value attached to them. Now if they were Russian orgies, they would be worth a fortune, because no Russian orgy has ever been filmed. To tell you the truth, we don't even know if they've ever had any since Rasputin. However, our books are Swedish, and we must move fast, or we may find ourselves in trouble. Now, Jack, what time can you leave tonight?'

'About nine.'

'Fine. Now, Father, here is what you must do. Pack the books in a tea chest and put something on top of them— bricks or Bibles or something, just in case the car is stopped by the police for some reason or other. I need the car until nine anyway, so I'll pick up the tea chest in the early evening, Father, and Jack can get my keys when he's ready. I'll be at Manor House with my parents and with Beatrice, unless I can think of something else to do with her. So there's no problem about finding me at home.'

'What about the contraceptives?' asked Father Scraw, not wishing them to be discovered in his house by chance now that he had attained a niche in the ecclesiastical hierarchy.

'I'll take them and sell them privately for a few extra pounds—every penny counts in the drive to save the steeple.'

'Agreed,' said Father Scraw.

'Superb,' said Jack.

'We go tonight,' said Sheaffer.

11

'TONIGHT, is it?' asked the Prime Minister, turning to his secretary.

'Tonight, sir,' confirmed Miss Kelly. 'Cartwright telephoned this morning before leaving for Scotland. He plans to strike tonight, just in case this Sheaffer fellow tries to smuggle them out of the country.'

'Might have done it already,' groaned the Prime Minister pessimistically, taking an indigestion tablet from the bottle on his desk. Middle Eastern dishes had never agreed with him; still, he had to make guests feel at home –even the Arabs. He swallowed some water and tried to feel better. 'You do have the Inland Revenue schedule there, Miss Kelly?'

'Sir.'

'Then schedule Cartwright for the difficult sums department,' he continued, stroking his well-shaven chin with narcissistic glee. 'But write it down in pencil—after all, there's just a chance he might succeed.'

There's just a chance I might succeed, thought Cartwright as he walked down the gangway from the aeroplane. Travelling had always adversely affected his optimism, and even an hour's flight from London diverted his thoughts from his plans and the inklings of success that accompanied them. Luxury always brought out the worst in him; adversity, the best. But flying was a curiously nondescript mixture of both conditions, and he had no love for it. He still harboured secret fears in his heart that every plane he flew in was destined to crash.

'Isn't it lovely, Cartie?' said Lucy Frome huskily, as they walked the short distance across to the arrival lounge. Hills shrouded in cloud lay in the misty beyond, and near-green fields spread out on either side of the quiet airport.

'No,' replied Cartwright, 'there's nothing lovely about it at all. That's Scotland, my dear. Looks pretty from a distance, but wait until you get there. Mist and snow, hail and rain the rest of the time. And nothing but miles of bloody moors and freezing streams. Scotland is the most uncivilised country in the world, except for Peru.'

'I've never been to Peru.'

'Neither have I,' said Cartwright, 'and I don't intend to go there.'

Cartwright did not add that he had never been to Scotland, either, and, intelligent though he was, he still had partially formed notions that kilts were worn by a substantial proportion of the population and that porridge and haggis formed the staple diet of the rural and industrial working class. Not that his preconceptions were so strong that he would be surprised when they were not fulfilled. He didn't really have preconceptions about anything at the moment; and all he wondered was how he was going to get to Lindenlee. Thinking, as he did, that this would be a comparatively simple matter, he closed his mind to the world and to women. Had the Queen of Sheba been sitting on his lap and feeding him sugared olives, he would have told her to screw off. The Queen of Sheba—well, perhaps he would have employed a less severe tone of dismissal; perhaps not; what the fuck; all he wanted was a cup of tea.

But there was no tea to be found in the arrival lounge. In

fact, there were hardly any people in the arrival lounge. The businessmen on the flight had all been whipped off by chauffeur-driven cars to town and city centres. Cartwright had no chauffeur.

'Couldn't we get a police car?' suggested Lucy.

'No,' said Cartwright, 'the police and the Secret Police have never got on. They dislike us because we get free trips to foreign countries, because we don't have to wear those horrible uniforms, and because we can carry guns and they can't. We'll wait for our luggage, then hire a car.'

A porter approached.

'Ah'm sorry, sir,' he said, in a rich Kirkcaldy accent, and not looking in the least bit sorry, 'but yer luggage is lost. It's either gone tae Istunbool or tae Paris.'

'Rubbish,' said Cartwright, thinking of every possible form of abuse in his vocabulary. 'Disgraceful, hideous— the sort of thing I expect from British Railways. Good God, man, do you realise the enormity of this? My luggage gone —everything! Dear Jesus bloody Christ all-fucking mighty —it has everything in it—my money, my gun . . .'

'God—a gun!' exclaimed the porter, as if he had beheld the Devil caressing the Holy Grail. 'Ye canny carry guns in ayeroplanes.'

'I am a secret policeman,' blurted Cartwright, turning many colours in various stages of extreme rage. 'Heads will fall for this. It will be like the Reign of Terror once more. Your planes will never fly again.'

The porter, who had never approved of Tom Sawyer taking the cane for Becky Thatcher, shrugged his shoulders and walked off towards a room marked STAFF ONLY.

Cartwright said, 'Fuck.'

'I know, dear,' said Lucy sympathetically, smiling like a lawyer who has just lost a suit she expected to win.

'Right,' said Cartwright with determination. Once more the chips were down. Lodged in hotels in the Bahamas he had made errors a child of six would not make in a nursery rhyme. But stuck in the slums of Paris he had befuddled spies from every corner of the globe. Adversity frowned on him once more and found him at his best. The path to Lindenlee was not a well-laid one. Most of his money lay in Istanbul, or wherever his bag had vanished to. Hiring a car was now out of the question. But he knew he would get there.

'How do we get to Lindenlee?' he asked a passing stranger.

'Never heard of it,' replied the passing stranger.

Neither had the next seven people Cartwright asked. The eighth had. 'Take the bus,' he said. 'It's the only way.'

They took a taxi to the bus station. That, at least, they could still afford.

'I'll get the tickets,' he said when they reached it. 'Get some change at the book stall, Lucy—then we can phone Amanda and tell her when we'll be there.' Cartwright went to the ticket office. 'The next bus,' he snapped. 'When's the next bus to Lindenlee?'

'There are no buses to Lindenlee,' replied the woman behind the desk, 'but there is a bus to Lincluden. That's three miles away. You can hitch the rest of the way.'

'When does it leave?'

'In two hours,' replied the woman.

'Nothing before?'

'Nothing at all,' said the woman.

'Ridiculous,' said Cartwright, preparing to spit on the floor, but just in time he remembered what his mother had taught him about good manners.

'How long does it take to get there?'

'Three hours,' replied the woman, looking pleased with herself and with the anger she was arousing in Cartwright.

'*Three hours?*' repeated Cartwright, deliberately and incredulously. '*Three hours* to travel *twenty-eight miles?* I don't believe it.'

'You don't have to,' said the woman.

'In that case,' said Cartwright, 'show me where the cafeteria is. God, I need a cup of tea.'

'Oh, we don't have a cafeteria,' said the woman, as if she had been deeply offended at the suggestion. 'We only have buses.'

'That travel,' said Cartwright, 'at nine miles an hour.'

'We don't like to hurry things up here,' said the woman in her low drowsy voice, which suggested that she practised what she preached. 'Remember, you're in Scotland now.'

Cartwright did not have to remember very hard.

12

BEATRICE had the afternoon off, which was lucky for Cartwright when he telephoned. He spoke to her for five minutes, exhorting her to action and subtle moves for the recovery of the vital condoms. She was to pave the way for the maestro. She was to root out this Sheaffer and discover where he lived and who his friends were.

'I already have,' she told him passively.

'You have!'

'I'm going out with him tonight.'

Cartwright uttered several words expressing great amazement and praise.

'Well done,' he concluded joyfully, and added in a note of caution, 'Do be careful.'

'I always am,' she said as she gently replaced the receiver. Then she walked out into the garden and transplanted some young leeks to use for soup when winter came. Green-fingered Beatrice. What a history of horticultural success lay behind her. How she had stormed the flower shows of Somerset in her youth, winning every section from the baby turnips to the giant marrow! Cups and medals embellished her bedroom furniture; scripts and scrolls covered the walls. She had been dedicated once, and these were an everlasting testament to that dedication.

Years ago the boys had gathered round on the way from school seeking her favour and sweet words of encouragement; she had left them at the gate and gone to the green-house. Skirt shed for jeans, blouse for an Aran sweater; the trowel was mightier than the pen, or a boy's first sticky kiss; after all, what was a cluster of sycophants to the clustered stalks of green on the head of a crisp celery stick. Boys were nice on Saturday; weekdays, the garden won. Men and women came from all around to seek advice from Beatrice. She taught them onion power, carrot strength, radish-rearing on sandy soil. Sometimes the men tried sweet talk; she talked tomatoes and organic fertilisers.

Her picture appeared in the newspapers on summer Saturdays. Beatrice the champ. She played the champ too, and she loved it. The boys didn't. Beware of Beatrice; Beatrice can cut you down. Beatrice did; and Beatrice lost out, in the end. Boys became more important, but Beatrice became less important to the boys. Everyone went drinking now on Saturday nights, everyone, that was, who was eighteen. Not Beatrice; the boys had nothing more to do with her; they were afraid of 'sorry buts' and 'I'd really love to but I can'ts'. She would have, though. But no one asked.

So Beatrice mended her ways. She made herself personable and, in time, it had become a habit, after a while unavoidable. The boys came back, but then it was time to leave for college. And there she met Raymond. Raymond was handsome and poor; all he had were five suède jackets, which he wore on different days of the week, except for the weekends, which he spent, in bed, with Beatrice. Beatrice was in love with Raymond. He was a strange mixture of arrogance and humility; he thought he was going to be the best occupational therapist in the world; and he wanted to help people. He didn't help Beatrice much, though. He left her for a rich doctor called Virginia, who was partial to suède jackets and bright young occupational therapists. Virginia left Ray-

mond a week later, causing him to burn all his jackets; then
he had nothing. Neither had Beatrice. A broken heart. How
foolish she had been to break out from the cosy security of
the greenhouse! She moped for weeks and ate nothing but
rhubarb crumble and custard. Then she graduated without
honours and went to work in Scotland, the only place in
Britain that occupational therapists without honours could
get a job. But the patients in the hospital were not very
therapeutically minded. Time hung on her hands like a bag
of wet sand. She decided to become a spy.

That was fun; Dumfries to London, and then to Lindenlee. No boys, of course, but they could wait. Painful memories of good-for-nothing Raymond still lingered in occasional
thoughts, like a small sharp stone in her shoe. Then there
was Sheaffer. Handsome, rich, and oh-so-mysterious. Present at Harold Wilcox's death, along with Father Scraw.
Old Tiger Wilcox, the best spy the country had produced in
half a century, put away by a mad priest and an eccentric
sectologist. Somehow it just didn't seem real. Something
was definitely up—that was why she had gone to the church
last night. And Sheaffer had often brought up altar wine
from London, had he? Once too often, perhaps. Still, it was
a big perhaps. After all, they didn't look like ruthless enemy
agents. But then, ruthless enemy agents never did. One
thing, anyway: she wasn't going to get all hot and bothered
about it. There was a solution to everything, even love.
Cartwright plunged into everything like a possessed lem-
ming. Gardening had taught Beatrice patience and expecta-
tion. Seeds that grew too quickly, like Raymond, were like
the ones in the parable of the sower—they withered and
died while the sun shone bright. Sheaffer hadn't even had
his first watering yet, in her book; so if he turned out to be a
bad apple, she wasn't going to starve. Yet something was

definitely very amiss. Mrs. Wilcox didn't need her to work that night; no one ever drank in a Scottish pub on a Monday evening. The poor spent all their money at the weekend; the moderately well-off spent some and saved the rest; and the rich drank in their homes. Beatrice was no fool. Someone had asked that she work. And that someone must be Sheaffer. Why? she wondered. Perhaps he just didn't fancy her any more; the aquiline nose, possibly? Be honest with yourself, girl, she thought—it's not aquiline; it's just plain big. Still, there might be a reason more flattering than that one. Perhaps a great symposium of modern sectologists had been called at short notice. But most probably it was a job he was pulling—a big job—*the* big job. But even then, how sure could she be? Only one person did she think she could trust, who could help her—the only girl in Lindenlee she could call a friend. She went inside, lifted the telephone, and asked the operator to put her through to Suzie Elliot.

13

HEATHROW airport was busy; Heathrow airport was always busy. In VIP lounge 1 the Prime Minister was forcing fond farewells on the Middle Eastern dignitary and smiling mouthfuls of teeth at the BBC television camera by the door.

'You will do *something*?' said the Middle Eastern dignitary, lifting his briefcase.

'Perhaps,' said the Prime Minister, in broken Arabic. 'We shall see,' he added, and dismissed the meeting entirely from his mind.

Two doors off, in VIP lounge 2, Ernest Sheaffer was smoking a cigar and thinking about bed and a few drinks. Ethel Sheaffer slowly sipped a cup of cocoa.

'Will it be cold, dear?' she asked her husband in a low, supplicating voice that did not quite amount to a whimper.

'Lindenlee, *no*—Antarctica, *yes*,' said Ernest. 'You see, dear, it has to be cold in those parts. I was reading only last night that if the polar caps melted, the world would be completely flooded. So it just has to be cold.'

'I see, dear,' replied Ethel Sheaffer, who didn't. She straightened her skirt and combed a loose hair into place. A good-looking woman for fifty, she thought, trying to admire her features in a pocket mirror; but what would Antarctica do to them? Frostbite, chilblains, frozen fingers, and that horrible disease you caught from looking at the snow for too long—what was it?—ah yes, the bends. She hoped that keeping igloo would not be too much for her. Still, Ernest knew best. The change in climate would do them both good.

An air hostess approached and told Mr. Sheaffer that his luggage was three tons overweight.

'How much are we allowed?' he asked.

'Forty-four pounds,' the hostess replied.

'What ones are causing the trouble?' asked Ernest, putting his feet up on a nearby chair.

'All of them,' replied the hostess, 'but two in particular. The ones marked TRINKETS FOR THE ESKIMOS and ROCK BUNS FOR THE POLAR BEARS.'

Ernest Sheaffer's Antarctic aide approached.

'Excuse me, sir,' he whispered, as he thought all good aides should, 'I forgot to tell you. There are no Eskimos or polar bears in those parts. You only get them at the other end.'

'Then send the trinkets somewhere in Africa, and the buns to London Zoo,' said Mr. Sheaffer, who liked to think he had an answer for everything. He turned to his aide. 'You're fired, Watkins,' he said.

'Thank you very much, sir,' said Watkins, who had been contriving at dismissal on any grounds for some time.

'With those packets removed, sir, the bill for excess luggage comes to one thousand four hundred pounds and eight pence.'

'Thank you,' said Ernest. 'Arithmetic was never my forte. I'll send you a cheque.' He turned to his wife.

'Hope that the boy's not working too hard,' she sighed.

'Needs a good drink in him,' said Ernest. 'And more sleep. Sleep never hurt a man. Good for the bowels.'

'You are *awful*, dear.'

'I know,' Ernest replied, 'but my family have let me down. I am the last degenerate Sheaffer. The son who will take my place is an abstemious eunuch.'

'What does that mean, dear?' she asked, managing a whimper this time and flickering her eyebrows in ostensible bewilderment.

Ernest sighed. 'He has a lot of catching up to do,' he replied.

In VIP lounge 3, the huge form of a man in late middle age, perfectly preserved, with iron muscle, slowly and deliberately paced the thick vermilion carpet. Occasionally he paused by a flimsy coffee table to take giant gulps from a twelve-ounce glass filled with Scotch. The man was thinking about crumpets, and about just how much at that moment he would love to taste a deliciously hot home-made crumpet spattered with strawberry jam. He also wished the floor of the lounge had no carpet, for he liked to hear the clump of his boots as he contemplated the meaning of pleasure.

The door opened, and an airline official told him the flight would depart in ten minutes. He snarled happily, as a man-eating gorilla would in Piccadilly Circus.

'Just one thing,' he said to the airline official. 'Get me a taxi at the other end.'

'To where, sir?' the official asked.

'To Lindenlee,' replied the enormous man without hesitation, 'and make it a fast one.'

14

PROFESSOR SWISH'S office was small, neat, dark, and irregularly shaped—rather like Professor Swish, who, at three o'clock on a now sunny Monday afternoon, was sitting at his desk chewing cashew nuts and filling out his entry for *Who's Who*.

'Swish, Oscar J.,' he wrote, 'historian, sectologist, novelist, philosopher.' He deleted 'philosopher'; not yet anyway, he thought. 'Educated Rugby, Oxford, and Harvard. Married Edith Frump, seven children (5b, 2g)." What a pity it had not been 5g and 2b. 'Regius professor of history and sectology at the University of Lindenlee', he continued. Under 'Publications', he wrote, '*A Concise History of Sects in Ten Volumes; A Day in the Life of a Bogomil; Manichaean Madness; Satanic Studies; Understanding Umbrians; Introducing Iconoclasm.*' He paused for another nut and continued, 'Under the pseudonym Iris Rose: *They Met in Moonlight; Marjorie and the Lonely Shepherd.* Under the pseudonym Grip Macsween: *A Poker in the Groin; No Coffin for Carmen; The Gouging of Gloria's Guts.*'

The telephone buzzed. 'Mr. Sheaffer to see you, sir.'

He scribbled 'shark-hunting' and 'tennis' under the entry for 'Hobbies' and slipped the form into a desk drawer.

As Sheaffer entered the office, Professor Swish rose and spoke as if he had been guzzling pots of honey from the age of six.

'Good to see you, Sheaffer,' he said.

My mentor, thought Sheaffer, and said, 'You too, sir,' with meaning.

'Take a seat—have a nut—a cigar, perhaps?'

. . . Thought he had plenty of money already . . .

'You're very kind, sir, I'll have a cigar.'

Sheaffer lit the cigar with a porcelain lighter in the shape of a Waldensian heretic.

'How are you?' asked Professor Swish, searching the surface of his mind for inoffensive gambits.

'Very much the same as ever, sir,' Sheaffer replied.

'And your father?'

'He's going to Antarctica, sir—to get away from it all. He'll be here tonight.'

'Splendid.'

'We're having a party, sir. If you and Mrs. Swish would like to come?'

'Why surely, Sheaffer—I should love to meet Ernest again. It's been a long time.'

'He once published one of your books, sir, didn't he? What one was that?'

'I forget,' said Professor Swish, who remembered perfectly well. Clouds from his youth still hung over his head in certain *après-garde* circles. Once he had lived; now he lived properly; he had to; but it wasn't nearly such fun.

'You have been here for eight years, Sheaffer,' he said.

'Eight and a half, sir,' corrected Sheaffer.

'And you have seen many people come and go.'

'Sir.'

'And, I daresay, you will see many more.'

'Sir.'

'Has leaving Lindenlee ever occurred to you, Sheaffer?'

'No, sir.'

'Never?'

'No, sir.'

... Dismissal ... expulsion ... take away that bauble ... banishment ... one-time sectologist ...

'Good,' said Professor Swish.

Why? thought Sheaffer.

'You are wondering *why* I said that, are you not, Sheaffer?'

'Sir.'

'So am I,' replied Professor Swish. 'I have taught many indolent people in my life, Sheaffer, including Deasy—you do remember Deasy, Sheaffer, don't you? Failed to graduate with anything after seven years. You are different, Sheaffer.'

'Sir.'

'You have two highly creditable degrees.'

'Sir.'

'Yet you are the laziest person I have ever known, except for your father. I hope you don't take that as an insult.'

'In our family, sir,' Sheaffer replied, 'we are encouraged to look on such comments as observations of the highest praise.'

'Good.'

'Sir.'

'But you are also the brightest person I have ever taught.'

Sheaffer picked himself up off the floor, straightened his chair, and sat down once more.

'I am going to offer you a job, Sheaffer.'

'Sir.'

'As an assistant lecturer and tutor in sectology.'

There was another loud noise.

'Sit over here, Sheaffer—this armchair is more stable.'

'Sir.'

'Well, Sheaffer, how do you feel?'

'Deeply moved, sir.'

'Then would you like the job?'

'Sir.'

'No problems, then—you can start next week?'

'One problem, sir. My father has always disapproved of my getting a job of any kind. If, perhaps, you could speak to him tonight . . .'

'Certainly,' replied Professor Swish. 'Delighted.'

'I can't tell you, sir.'

'I realise that, Sheaffer, but try harder.'

'How moving this is, sir. Sectology is my life. I eat, sleep, and drink it, sir.'

'Along with other beverages, I don't doubt,' said Professor Swish. 'You realise you cannot drink in classes, Sheaffer?'

'I don't mind, sir—this could be the first step to sectological success. I'll sacrifice everything, sir.'

'And of course you can't go spending all summer in Provence and Easter in Geneva. You will have to spend some of the time here, preparing for classes.'

'Anything, sir.'

'Then you may consider yourself a professional sectologist, Sheaffer—assuming your father approves.'

The office spun around Sheaffer in many colours. He left in a state of suspended consciousness. Go whereso'er I may, he thought, by night or day, the things that I have done, I now will do no more. After tonight, that is.

15

She was waiting for him now, naked and ready, her heart beating loudly, her legs spread wide asunder.

'Fuck me,' she screamed.

'I will,' he replied, smirking, as he thumped his long pounding throbber home.

FATHER SCRAW paused; a thin wisp of a smile drifted across his lips; he returned *The Seduction of Olga* to the massive tea chest in his attic and scratched his head lightly. How times had changed, he thought. Nothing of that sort written in his day. Seduction of Olga indeed; she hadn't taken much seducing, that was for sure. All that stuff about legs asunder and pounding throbbers; he supposed it must mean—yes, it couldn't possibly mean anything else. Well, his throbber hadn't done much pounding for a while; not that it ever had throbbed much anyway, or been all that long. Still, how did he know that? Apart from a curious glance at his father in the toilet once, when he was little, he had no idea what other men boasted; but they always seemed enormous in dirty books. Perhaps, he thought, with no great enthusiasm, he himself had been endowed with the greatest ever; the biggest throbber of them all. What if news of his endowment had spread across the land and women had flocked to Lindenlee craving him? That might have been fun; then again, it might have been quite embarrassing. Scraw the Stud, that's what they would have called him. Look, girls, there goes the lusty Scraw. Sexy Scraw, seeking out the choir girls and sweet-talking them in the vestry. No, it was not for him, none of it. Whatever God had given him had been sparingly used; perhaps too sparingly, but then again, it paid not to overdo it, even if you weren't a priest. If you weren't too careful, you might catch that awful disease that mariners caught—what was it?—ah, yes, the bends. Father Scraw felt very glad he had never had the bends. Delius had died of that, so too had Van Gogh. No. He shot himself in a cornfield, silly man; or was that Napoleon? Anyway, it was a Frenchman, or a Dutchman; possibly even a flying Dutchman. Scraw, he thought, the Flying Priest; communion in the air; probably, he mused, they have flying priests in Australia. They had everything in Australia, and in Africa too. Soon they would have flying priests in dear old Scotland, dotted across the sky. That was progress for you. Thank God he would not live to see it.

Father Scraw looked across at the last book in the cardboard wine boxes and placed it on top of the tea chest. *Torrid Tessy*, it was called, in full 'seductive' colour. He placed the contraceptives next to *Torrid Tessy* and made a mental note to remove them and give them to Sheaffer under separate wrapping. Then he reached into a sack on his left and began covering up the pornographic offerings with dilapidated hymnaries. Perhaps, he thought, in this den of iniquity to which these books are bound, some man of passion might find a hymnary and a new life. As long as it wasn't too new—newly converted Christians were always the worst.

For Father Scraw, then, Christianity was a passive religion, to be sipped, and not swallowed piecemeal. It was, he decided, an osmotic process. Osmotic, now that was a good word. His place in history was marked. Read Scraw for tomorrow, professors would say; his osmotic theory is baffling to all. There would be a plaque on his wall and another on the ground below—which saints might praise and infidels adore; and dogs urinate on. What a pity, he thought, that death almost invariably precedes fame. Still, he had lived without it for long enough now. At least they had made him a bishop.

Father Scraw fitted the lid on the tea chest as silently as possible and decided he would buy a bright green mitre that afternoon. What fun it was being a bishop at last; even more fun to look like one and bless himself in the bathroom mirror. He descended the attic stairs with extreme caution, crept out of the house before his wife could ensnare him for some disagreeable chore, and drove to Edinburgh and to Sam's Spiritual Supermarket.

16

THE carpet on the living-room floor of Suzie Elliot's fisherman's cottage was ochre-yellow, partly worn, patched in places, but clean all over. Suzie had been dusting out the fisherman's cottage all afternoon, polishing the brasses and the tables, wiping the ornaments on the mantelpiece, and taking the vacuum cleaner to everything that displayed the faintest trace of dirt; over almost everything, that was. Now it was finished; for two glorious days everything would be placed meticulously where it belonged. And then, once more, the gradual slide to untidiness would start, fostered by herself, aided by Sheaffer and by the host of friends who came for her coconut buns and other delicacies. Suzie was proud of her cleaning, as are most people who don't clean up very often, and consequently she was heartened and encouraged when it was the first thing Beatrice mentioned on her arrival. Suzie told Beatrice it was wonderful to see her; and so it was. Beatrice returned the compliment. Now they could polish off a freshly baked batch of coconut buns between them. Well, not quite polish them all off— some, at least, must be left for Sheaffer's father, who, Suzie said, was a connoisseur of coconut buns and had once, in an uncharacteristic wave of industry, made some himself.

'I didn't know his father was coming,' said Beatrice when they had sat down by the log fire, each with a bun in one hand and a steaming cup of jasmine tea in the other. 'And I didn't know about the party, either.'

'Actually, he forgets,' said Suzie, sighing. 'He has an awful memory. But if he's taking you out, he's bound to take you to it. In fact, he's sure to be madly in love with you already. That's one of his problems, you see—he falls in love with every girl he goes out with, and lots more that he doesn't have the courage to ask out; except for me, that is.'

'Lucky me,' replied Beatrice, in a not unsarcastic tone of voice.

'Oh, you are,' said Suzie with conviction, another bun in her hand. 'He's intelligent, he's handsome, and he's rich—he's fun-loving too, and he's generous—and on top of everything else, eccentric. That probably sums him up best. But, you see, the problem is, he has this terrible sex hang-up.'

'What kind of a hang-up?' asked Beatrice. The sixty-four-thousand-dollar question: horny or a gelding? She couldn't guess which.

'Well,' said Suzie, lowering her voice and leaning towards Beatrice, 'to tell you the truth, I don't think he's ever had it. He says he has, and that he's just lost interest. But frankly speaking, and drawing on my extensive experience with many men of different creeds, nationalities, and hang-ups, I don't think he would even know how to begin.'

'You mean he's a . . .'

'A virgin,' said Suzie, nodding vigorously, as if she had just discovered a new name for excrement, 'possibly even the type who goes out with the boys and talks about all the women he's laid and how he's sick of doing it and doesn't care any more. I think he has doubts about his ability in bed. In short, I think he's frigid. And we both know, Beatrice, that there's only one remedy for frigidity, and that's practice.'

Beatrice winked in reply and thought of unworthy Raymond.

'So you don't have to worry about being raped. That's the trouble, really, with these rich men. They always ask you first, and there's no fun in that. Mutual spontaneity—that's what I like.'

'Me too,' replied Beatrice, whose affair with Raymond had consisted almost entirely of mutually spontaneous episodes. Then she thought for a bit while Suzie made some more tea. A sexless Sheaffer—that really was a shock. But what was his game? Could she find out? She was going to try, anyway. 'He wanted me to work tonight, Suzie,' she said, trying to be passive about it but exuding indignation. 'What's he playing at?'

'He doesn't want you to meet his parents,' Suzie replied. 'You see, his parents both want him to get married to ensure that there will be an heir for the toothpaste empire. But his mother is very holy and always drops hints about the glorious sacrament of marriage whenever she meets him and he's with a girl. I had all that guff for years—but, of course, it never came to anything. You see, I used to live next to them in London, before my father took to drinking as a profession. As for Sheaffer's father—well, I mean, he used to publish dirty books. He's a dirty old bugger and no mistake. No one knows why he married Ethel, but she converted him. I think it was a sad tale of love at first sight.'

Beatrice felt a little better; at least her aquiline nose wasn't to blame for Sheaffer's prevaricative behaviour. Something else troubled her deeply, though, naturally enough. 'About Harold Wilcox,' she said suddenly. 'Sheaffer, Father Scraw, and a man called Ernie Green were playing dominoes when he died. Tell me, Suzie, is that the true story?'

Suzie nodded earnestly.

'But listen,' Beatrice continued, 'does anyone know *why* he died?'

'You don't think they *killed* him?'

'Of course not,' said Beatrice, hedging. 'It just crossed my mind.'

'Well,' said Suzie, lowering her voice once more, as if the ghost of the old fisherman, dead but a week, might have returned to haunt his former home, 'if I tell you something, will you promise me you'll never tell a single solitary soul?'

Beatrice promised, and crossed her heart intently.

'Well,' said Suzie, giggling, and raising her arms high in the air, 'it's really very simple. Harold Wilcox isn't dead.'

17

NOR was he. At that very moment, thousands of feet above the face of the earth, the monstrous form of Harold Wilcox, with arms of iron and chest of steel, heaved and sighed in his first-class plane seat. Even first-class seats were not big enough to hold Harold Wilcox. His muscular legs, still leather-tough and powerful despite his sixty years, were pinned to the inner wall of the plane. On the tray before him sat a glass of Scotch and a bottle of Campbell's extra-strong special brew—his fifth bottle of the trip, and not likely to last him much longer, either. An experienced steward, fast on his feet, had, in fact, been assigned to look after Harold, and he spent his time dashing between the bar and his charge. At this rate, Harold thought, by the time he reached Linden-lee he would be in the most desirable condition in the world: suspended inebriation. How glorious it would be to guzzle a muffin once more, or a crumpet, to sit in his bar or in the toilet and drink to his heart's content with the knowledge that he did not have to pay for it. Still, he had no problem with money now, and never would again. He could even give up the bar. But why do that when there was, within the confines of a public house, all that any normal man of sixty would need for the rest of his days?

Then Harold thought of football matches and exciting goals, of speeding in his van as he went to pick up more kegs

from the brewery, of spending Sunday in bed with a newspaper, and of walks on the beach with only his pocket flask
and Noah, his dog, to keep him company.

Harold finished off his Scotch and gulped down the rest
of his beer in one prodigious swallow. 'Steward,' he called
animatedly, 'another Campbell's please.'

It was in his hand in an instant. He wrenched the top from
the bottle with his bare hand and an expression of something more than glee. This, he thought, was life.

Five seats down from Harold Wilcox, Ernest Sheaffer was
trying to snooze.

'Will there be churches in Antarctica, dear?' his wife
asked timidly.

'Don't know,' he replied drowsily. 'If not, I'll build you
one.' Thinking better of this last remark, he turned to his
valet.

'Frank,' he snapped, rousing him with a sharp nudge on
the shoulder, 'have you ever built a church before?'

'I don't think so, Ernie.'

'Well, you'd better buy a book on it when we get to Lindenlee. Ethel wants a church, and we must placate her.
Your Myrtle can use it too, if she wants.'

'Thank you, dear,' said Ethel Sheaffer; she fell asleep,
and dreamed of penguins; the engines droned on.

Meanwhile, on the bumpy winding road to Lindenlee, an
exasperated bus driver chewed some black tobacco as his bus
stood motionless in a lay-by.

'Are ye finished yet?' he shouted angrily through the
open door of his vehicle.

'Not *quite* yet,' came a woman's plaintive voice, which

was followed by unhappy retchings and pained gurgles. Then a very dirty word was heard as Cartwright finished depositing the remains of a ham sandwich on an unsuspecting clump of clover.

18

DUSK was creeping into Lindenlee, the briskness of the afternoon was gone; the day was clammy now, almost sticky, and grey cumulus clouds clotted the sky. The sand on the beach was swirling low, and, swept by a rising wind, it filtered along the narrow streets by the sea, into shoes and socks, eyes and noses, hair. The sea itself roared loud with waves, muffled by the wind. The flags on the golf courses fluttered and snapped; the pins began to bend, and soon the wind whistled across the links, snapping small twigs from broken bracken or fading gorse. In the town centre, the town-hall bell tolled five. Shoppers scurried home to warm fires and waterproof houses; everyone knew it—storm, gale, thunder; pattering rain would soon be splashing the pavements; crackling lightning; church steeples rocking in the wind; and Father Scraw's steeple might even fall down.

Such was the thought that occurred to Sheaffer as he walked home from David's Delicatessen. Sheaffer adored storms; there was something rather wonderful about getting really wet, especially when you knew you could be home in the bathtub, all warm and cosy, in five minutes. He hoped the lightning wouldn't stave off for too long; it was so exciting, seeing the sky all ripped up. The power, he thought, of nature. . . . The feeble powers of man exposed . . . thunder . . . stormy seas . . . This is your captain speaking . . . abandon ship . . . lower the boats . . . Don't be a fool, Cap-

159

tain Sheaffer . . . she cannot be saved . . . Staying with my ship, MacTavish . . . England's pride and glory . . . Davy Jones will look after me. . . . But, Captain, you owe it to sectology . . . and to Admiral Beatrice . . . Tell her I died bravely, MacTavish . . . tell her I was happy till the last. . . . When men speak of Drake and Nelson, do not let them forget the name of Sheaffer. . . . Kiss me, MacTavish. . . .

'Watch where you're going, young man,' said an old woman.

'Sorry,' said Sheaffer, helping the old woman up off the ground. . . . Poor old soul . . . probably scared for her life . . . hiding under the bed . . . not me . . . should have been a lifeboat man . . . Fetch young Sheaffer, men; he'll save them all with spirit. . . .

Suddenly the sky was shredded by a long treelike flash of lightning. The thunder was almost overhead. In front of him, Sheaffer could see a huge sign, advertising Campbell's extra-strong special keg, swaying in the wind. Beside the sign was another board, on which an animal that was supposed to be a donkey was crudely painted; the donkey seemed to be in considerable pain.

So was Mrs. Wilcox when Sheaffer went inside. She had picked her nose once too often, and, although the bleeding had subsided, a nagging pain remained.

Sheaffer handed her the parcel he had brought from the delicatessen. 'I got this for the party, Miriam,' he said. 'Isn't it a wonderful night?'

'Wonderful, I'm sure,' said Mrs. Wilcox, wincing as her overpicked nose hurt yet again. She paused and yawned, poured a Guinness for Sheaffer, and returned to her favourite conversational topic. 'How much more wonderful it would be,' she said, looking decidedly morose, 'if my dear old Harold hadn't been taken in such a terrible way only one year ago, him that loved the Guinness even more than yourself. Guinness buns and scones I used to make for him—and Guinness crumpets. Lord, how he adored his Guinness crumpets. Took Guinness with everything, my Harold. Why, he'd even have it in his porridge and his rice pudding if I didn't get in there with the milk first.'

'A tragedy indeed,' said Sheaffer, 'but at least we know he died a happy man.'

'No *so* happy,' said Mrs. Wilcox, screwing her face up and with the knowledge that she knew something Sheaffer didn't. 'He would have been happier still if I'd been freer with him than I was in his latter days, God bless his soul, for he needs to, my God. Mind you, I know there was a time when he was even hornier, but it's better for men to get all that sex out of them before they settle down. Always on about it he was, to begin with, but I soon put a stop to that, so I did. I just told him; "Harold," I said, "don't you go expecting me to be . . . well, you know . . . just when you happen to feel like it. It's different for us women, Harold," I said; "we don't always get worked up the way you do. And if you think I'm putting down this knitting to get down in front of the fire, just because you've seen some half-dressed whore in the paper, then you're wrong." But he was a good man, my Harold, and soon got out of those dirty habits. Although not quite. None of you do,' she concluded with a flourish, pointing her index finger accusingly in the direction of Sheaffer's testicles.

'Sex means nothing to me,' said Sheaffer predictably. 'I burned myself out in my youth.' He gulped his Guinness quickly. Lots to do, he thought; besides which, he wanted to enjoy more of the storm outside. 'Must dash now,' he said, making for the door, his upper lip coated with Guinness foam. 'I'll see you tonight.'

Shutters were going up on windows that had them. Rain was patting quickly on the pavements, and the fading heat of a few minutes before was turning into a draughty coolness. Mist had begun to rise from the sea and ease down on the roofs of houses as he made his way slowly home, wondering if perhaps he had not burned himself out in his youth after all. Temptation eventually overcame him, and, pausing in a doorway, he took out the small box the doctor had given him and swallowed a sexule. Just as he realised the possible consequences of his action, the din of the wind and the slish of the rain were broken by a biting crack, a noise not dissimilar to an earthquake, and the ground trembled for several seconds beneath his feet. He knew at once that something very very heavy had fallen a very long way. And without straining his mind unduly, Sheaffer felt he had a very good idea what that something was.

19

'DEAD,' said Mrs. Danby-Walker-Jones, pursing her lips with restrained excitement. 'Scraw's dead.'

'Appalling,' said Mrs. MacWesterton, her mouth dripping with droplets of enthusiastic saliva.

' 'Fraid so, ladies,' mumbled a bored policeman. 'That's the last thing his dear wife said before they dragged her off to the hospital for a cup of tea. Lucky for her she was shopping at the time. Last seen in the attic, old Scraw. Dead as a doornail, he must be, and only just made a bishop too.'

'He was a good and noble man,' said Mrs. MacWesterton.

'Humble,' said Mrs. Danby-Walker-Jones, thinking it meant something else.

'Religious,' muttered Mrs. MacWesterton, who then realised the foolishness of her thoughtless remark. 'In the performance of his duties, I mean,' she added.

'Aye—it's sad,' said the policeman, thinking of hot bowls of country vegetable soup.

A large crowd had now gathered around the fallen steeple, which had exactly bisected the manse of All Saints Episcopal Church. Many stood silent, waiting for rumours; others heard rumours, exaggerated them, passed them on, and then thought of even worse things that might have happened. Father Scraw had been crushed to pulp. His head had been completely severed and had been found lying beside an open Bible. He had been praying when the steeple

163

struck. Someone had heard him scream 'I fear not death, my Lord' with his last breath. He had given all his money for building a new steeple. His funeral was to be a simple one, and he was to be buried in a quiet rural cemetery near his birthplace. No flowers were to be sent because of his hatred of ostentation; he wanted to die, as he had lived, in apostolic simplicity.

Meanwhile, on the Lindenlee Road, death was farthest from the thoughts of Father Scraw as he sped along in his jet-black Rover at breath-taking speed. Trucks and buses pulled aside as he approached; a bloody madman, their drivers thought; and they were not far from the truth. Father Scraw found great solace in driving fast, and despite many speeding offences, he had never killed or injured anyone except a Cheshire cat that had once run under the front wheel of a bicycle he was riding. What he adored most was driving in the rain. This gave him a great sense of his own importance; he felt he might have been an excellent rally driver, had chance and God so chosen him to be.

As he approached the village of Lincluden, however, Father Scraw slowed down. The roads were soaked and slippy, and the way through Lincluden was a twisting one; besides, there were always children about, even in the worst of weather. But Father Scraw did not slow down quickly enough. As he reached the first bend into the village, the front wheel of the Rover caught the left-hand kerb, and only an instinctive twist of the steering wheel saved him from destroying the local shop, the Rover, and himself. The car then checked and made a harsh disagreeable noise suggesting that something integral in the locomotive process had expired. Clouds of grey and yellow gases spewed from the exhaust as the car finally came to rest ten yards in front of a tired, distressed, and drenched-looking man and woman. Father Scraw leaped out nimbly, ran to the back of the Rover, and kicked the exhaust hard. The fumes immediately ceased to pour forth.

'I wonder,' asked Cartwright, with cautious optimism, 'if we could possibly scrounge a lift to Lindenlee?'

'That's why I stopped,' lied Father Scraw. He looked at the bedraggled, shivering figure of Lucy with the kind of compassionate smile that only elderly people who have lived can produce and said, 'You'd best go in the back, my dear—you can put your head down there.'

It was too dark now for Cartwright to see the obstacles on the road that Father Scraw just missed hitting. Soon the lights of Lindenlee shone in the distance, through the driving rain and the white sea mist, which seemed to thin and wisp as they approached the town.

'If you reach behind the seat there,' said Father Scraw to Cartwright, 'you will find something.'

Cartwright found a brown box with a piece of string around it and a tag that said SAM'S SPIRITUAL SUPER-MARKET.

'Open it, if you don't mind, and tell me what you think,' said Father Scraw.

Cartwright untied the string and opened the box. 'I don't know what it is,' he admitted reluctantly, in lethargic be-wilderment.

'Why, a mitre, of course,' said Father Scraw, as if it were as common a sight as a skinless sausage. 'I just got it today. Isn't it really superb? Emerald green—size seven.'

'You mean you're a . . .'

'A bishop,' interjected Father Scraw. 'I am one, in fact, but not officially until the ceremony, when I get the ring and staff. You always get the same ring and staff as the last bloke, but the church buys you a mitre, just in case the previous incumbent had worms or dandruff.'

'It was very kind of your Grace to . . .'

'No trouble at all,' said Father Scraw. 'Devilishly difficult place to get to, this. I only hope you enjoy your holiday. Where would you like me to drop you off?'

'The Crown Hotel, if you don't mind, your Grace,' Cartwright replied as they passed the first hotel on the Lindenlee waterfront.

'A pleasure,' said Father Scraw with great sincerity. 'You see, I always go there at this time myself. Perhaps, sir, you would pass me over my false-beard box. Hidden identity. I'm sure I can trust *you.*'

Cartwright did so without hesitation; nothing, he felt, would ever surprise him again, except perhaps a situation completely uncomplicated and entirely normal. He yawned; the urge for a drink was returning, and for sex, and violence; perhaps a little shooting; and some blood; or even a death, or two, or three. Cartwright felt himself again.

20

STREET lights were blurred and traffic at a standstill as Sheaffer guided the Mercedes slowly and precisely down Westfield Road, with a look of quiet determination on his face. Easing it into a tight space by the roadside, he got out quickly and closed the door. Through the ruins of the manse he could see firemen grunting as they lifted stones and rafters and peered beneath them in their search for the body of Father Scraw. Applied mathematics had never been Sheaffer's strong point, but now he grappled inventively with the problem of where the pornographic books could possibly have fallen—if they were still recognisable, that was. He sank to his knees and crawled uncomfortably on his stomach across the wet grass, nearer and nearer to the house, getting progressively more and more soaked and wondering just exactly how he was going to carry the things if he ever found them. Torches flashed in the ruins; the voices of the searchers rang in the air.

'Hadn't a chance,' said one man.

'At least it was quick,' said another.

Sheaffer looked to his right and saw part of a wardrobe smothered in long dresses; beside them was a broken toilet seat and part of the kitchen sink. Then there were a few bashed groceries—he put his hand on several eggs, and wiped his fingers clean on some wet leaves. To his left lay a heap of torn and sodden books that looked decidedly ecclesiastical and unpornographic; mounted on the books was a single boot and what looked like a can of sliced green beans. The situation seemed desperate; and then he saw them. God, what luck, he thought, but he immediately noticed that the chest had been partly split in its fall, and three or four books had escaped. I hope that was all, he thought as he stuffed them into his pockets. Now for the chest. He stood up ever so slowly, hoping that no torch would flash in his direction. The searchers, he was relieved to observe, seemed disheartened.

'Lucky if we find a leg, Bert,' said one.

'Hahahahahaha,' roared the other.

Sheaffer wanted to go over and strike the man, but decided that he might be much stronger; besides, he had work to do.

Unfortunately, there was no prospect of his being able to carry the case; so, concealing himself behind it, Sheaffer began rolling it backwards, one edge at a time. The case shuddered as he pulled at it jerkily, using all his inconsiderable strength; back once, then again, once more, then a quick rest.

'Might as well give up,' said one fireman to his mate.

Please do, thought Sheaffer, breathing more loudly than he wished to. He pulled the chest back another few feet; back again, then again; then it crunched on some already-broken pieces of china, one of which spurted up and just missed his eye. The chest landed on a metal coat hanger, which sprang at him and bit into his ankle. He squealed a sharp cry of pain.

'Someone out there, Bert,' said one fireman.

Sheaffer curled up behind the chest and froze.

'Still alive, p'rhaps,' said the searcher called Bert.

. . . God . . . like films . . . bayonets . . . pitchforks . . .

'I'm going to take a look, Bert. Could be the old bastard is dying out there,' said Bert's friend.

Sheaffer heard the heavy boots splashing in the muddy grass, coming towards him closer and closer, heavier and heavier; the squelching grew louder and louder; and Sheaffer knew his time had come.

21

THE situation, thought Beatrice, as she sat on the bed clipping her toenails, is very clear. In fact, there are only ten possible explanations for events up to now. She clipped the last nail, went to her desk, and scribbled down some random thoughts that had occurred to her since her meeting with Suzie Elliot.

1. Sheaffer killed Harold Wilcox with the help of Father Scraw. Then he made the funeral arrangements with Ernie Green, the town undertaker, who was present when Harold died. The body was then coffined and buried before anyone thought about a post-mortem.

Hence:

(a) Sheaffer is a spy working for the Russians. [At this point Beatrice imagined what Sheaffer would look like wearing a Cossack hat.]

(b) Father Scraw is a spy working for the Russians.

(c) Harold Wilcox knew that Sheaffer and Father Scraw were working for the Russians and that is why he died.

2. Sheaffer is the only spy and he killed Harold Wilcox single-handed. Father Scraw is Sheaffer's dupe.

3. Father Scraw is the only spy and he killed Harold Wilcox single-handed. Sheaffer is Father Scraw's dupe.

4. *Suzie's story* (told to her by Sheaffer):

Harold Wilcox couldn't stand living with Miriam Wilcox any longer because she picked her nose so often. This is logical, since I can't stand it after only four weeks there. Harold Wilcox asked

Sheaffer, Father Scraw, and Ernie Green to pretend he was dead. Then he escaped from the coffin and is now leading a new life elsewhere.

5. Suzie is not telling the truth, but, instead, she killed Harold Wilcox with cyanide and is trying to put the blame on someone else. However, this is unlikely since Suzie is such a nice girl and a good friend, and wouldn't want to kill Harold Wilcox anyway.

6. Harold Wilcox is, was, and always will be a double agent. He is alive and working with Sheaffer and Father Scraw. All are working for the Russians. [At this point Beatrice imagined all three with Cossack hats on.] The secrets are in Father Scraw's house or have already been destroyed by Wilcox, who is the mastermind.

7. Harold Wilcox died of *alcoholism*, which is logical, since he was an alcoholic. Sheaffer went to collect altar wine in London and picked up the wrong box, which he has since returned by post to London, and which will arrive there soon. Then all will be well.

Hence.

(a) Sheaffer is not a spy.

(b) Father Scraw is not a spy.

(c) Beatrice and Cartwright are wasting their time.

8. Sheaffer plans to kill everyone eventually, starting with me *tonight*.

9. Cartwright has gone insane and there never were any secrets at all.

Hence:

(a) Cartwright has been working too hard,

or

(b) Cartwright wants passionately to work for the Inland Revenue.

10. *Points to be taken into consideration:*

(a) Sheaffer is nice.

(b) Sheaffer is handsome.

(c) Sheaffer is intelligent.

(d) Sheaffer is very rich.

(e) Sheaffer is fun-loving.

(f) Sheaffer seems to like me.

(g) Beatrice would like to have a boy friend (although not necessarily Sheaffer).

(h) Beatrice is an awful spy.

(i) Beatrice should never have become a spy in the first place.

(j) Tomorrow, Beatrice is going to cease to be a spy—that is, if Beatrice is still alive.

Beatrice put down her pen and moaned in abject confusion. There was a knock on the door, and her flatmate, Sylvia, came in.

'Beatrice!' she exclaimed loudly. 'Beatrice, All Saints' steeple has fallen right on old Scraw's house, and everyone thinks he's had it.'

As if somehow he knew by instinct, Cartwright was on the spot once more. His capacity for proficiency when things looked their worst seemed almost inexhaustible.

The telephone rang in Beatrice's room, and he was at the other end of the line. 'They're in a church,' she blurted, 'a church that's just been destroyed.'

'Hold it there,' said Cartwright, his voice seething with uncontrollable enthusiasm and emotion, 'hold it right there, and I'll be with you in five minutes, Amanda. Prepare to lead me to this place. Our country's destiny lies in your hands.'

Beatrice was glad it was her country's destiny and not her own.

22

'The trouble with our son,' said Ernest Sheaffer, yawning, to pass the time, 'is that he never does anything except study.'

'He's a good boy,' his wife replied, crossing herself as the Rolls-Royce sped faster towards Lindenlee.

'Ten minutes more, and we're there,' said Ernest. 'A stiff gin, a chat, and then bed.' The only way, he thought, to pass a day.

'Gone?' rasped Cartwright, as he shook with fury beside the crumbled steeple of All Saints, with rain running down his back. 'Where the hell to?'

'To the station, sir,' the young policeman replied superciliously, 'along with a young man with only one name, who found them. I think,' he added, in a tone Cartwright found almost intolerably arrogant, 'that we may have found your man.'

Father Scraw's Guinness fell from his hand, spread like a huge ink blot across the bar of the Crown Hotel, and dripped to the tiled floor when Ernie Green told him he was supposed to be dead.

'Dead,' he gasped. 'And my steeple gone, my beautiful steeple. And my wife, what about her?'

'Alive and well,' said Ernie comfortingly, where comfort was not needed. 'But as for Sheaffer—a sorry case.'

'What . . . good Lord . . . what?' exclaimed Father Scraw, taking a sip of Ernie's drink and spilling some of it also. 'What happened to him?'

'Caught in the ruins,' said Ernie, shaking his head, 'stealing a chest, they say.'

'Dear Jesus Christ,' said Father Scraw in an uncharacteristic burst of blasphemy. He ran to the door of the bar, jumped into his car, and headed for the Lindenlee police station.

23

THE police station into which Sheaffer had been led was a very strange police station. It was small, dingy, thinly furnished, and looked rather like a badly equipped gymnasium in an impoverished public school; it also smelled of stale vegetables, carrots and turnips mostly. True, there was nothing unusual in that; yet there was also in the station a general unconcern about the ways of the world. Herbert, the only vigilant policeman there, whom Cartwright had encountered beneath the steeple, was ostracised by his fellow officers of law. No one else had arrested anyone in seven years, and no one intended to break the long tradition. For the past four annual police conventions, the Lindenlee Constabulary had been voted the best force in the country because they had simply stamped out all offences in the neighbourhood. Crime prevention was their motif; and since they could not prevent it they made a point of not noticing it when it occurred—unless, of course, someone ruthless or particularly undesirable was involved. Ruthless and undesirable people were, however, scarce in those parts, and only an occasional wife killer or speed fiend roamed the streets. Law did not have to be enforced in Lindenlee, and order reigned supreme. No one was bribed, because no one had to be. The police were happy, the public was happy, and the local jailer had turned the prison into a darts room for Youth Fellowship meetings. The cherished shield for the best police force in the country was there to stay, and only somebody terribly wicked could force the constables to get out their little black books, the pages of which had grown yellow through desuetude. The four policemen, with the exception of the vigilant Herbert, were all in late middle age and all of them had large red noses, genial expressions, and the sort of perpetual grins that suggested much of their lives had been spent performing simple deeds and charitable acts. Boredom descended leisurely upon their shoulders, as if it somehow anticipated a favourable reception, and for most of their time on duty the constables drank tea or stronger beverages, played cards, read the racing results, and occasionally told stories about their adventures before they had become policemen. Most of them had been to sea, and consequently their stories were often dirty ones. Accordingly, the contents of the tea chest that had accompanied Sheaffer to the station were well received and inexorably destined for confiscation, regardless of Sheaffer's fate.

Sheaffer's fate was, as it happened, no longer the uppermost thing in his mind. The proceedings of the day to date, culminating in his arrest, had dulled his thoughts and brought about that exotic feeling of carefree limpness which usually only follows a hot bath. Sitting, as he was, in a comfortable armchair, with a blanket around him, a newspaper in his lap, a cup of tea in one hand and a deck of cards in the other, he felt his initial nightmares about being hanged, drawn, quartered, and generally mutilated after years of hard labour in Siberia beginning to fade. Initially, he had been charged by the bright young constable Herbert with breaking and entering, breach of the peace, murder, handling pornographic works, and parking in a forbidden zone. However, Herbert had been quickly dispatched to guard the fallen steeple, and the sergeant at the desk had begun to think of ways in which Sheaffer's alleged offences might be reduced to manageable proportions. Meanwhile, everyone else, Sheaffer included, was playing whist.

'The problem,' said the old sergeant, sounding noble and inspired, 'is really not a problem at all.'

The policemen looked up from their cards and nodded in grave silence.

'Mr. Sheaffer,' the sergeant continued, in his deep and almost, though not quite, monotonous voice, 'is really a man of quite enormous spirit.'

Sheaffer concluded that this remark was on account of the series of ethnic and religious jokes he had told during the previous few minutes.

The policemen looked up once more, nodded their heads vigorously and mumbled 'man of spirit' several times.

'Besides which,' said the sergeant, raising his deep voice, 'Mr. Sheaffer was the victim of a young officer's overblown enthusiasm.'

'Hear, hear,' said one policeman.

Sheaffer took a half-bottle of Scotch from his coat pocket and offered it round. There were several more 'hear hear's, and then everyone said 'certainly' at the same time.

'Firstly,' said the sergeant, 'Mr. Sheaffer could not be guilty of breaking and entering because he was only in the garden at the time. And, in any case, the house was already broken and entered by the steeple when he arrived.'

'Definitely,' said two policemen.

The sergeant deleted 'breaking and entering' from the list of charges. 'Secondly,' he continued, 'the peace was already so disturbed by the storm by the time Mr. Sheaffer made his appearance that even a brass band could not have broken it.'

The policemen nodded their heads gravely in absolute agreement with their senior officer.

The sergeant deleted 'breach of the peace' from the list.

Sheaffer poured the sergeant an extra-large whisky in his empty teacup.

'Furthermore,' said the sergeant, his voice rising to a veritable fortissimo, 'no one has been murdered. There was no body. And Mr. Sheaffer has explained that Father Scraw was, in fact, busy shopping in an ecclesiastical supermarket at the time the steeple fell.'

There was a long silence after this remark, as trumps were won and lost.

'Well,' said the sergeant, '*was* anyone murdered?'

Four loud 'no's boomed across the room.

'Good,' said the sergeant, obviously happy at having his own way. 'And as for the pornography charge—well, are any of you men depraved and corrupted by what you have just seen in that tea chest?'

'Never,' roared the four voices once more.

'Neither am I,' said the sergeant, deleting 'murder' and 'handling pornographic works' from the charge list. 'But there is one other offence—parking in a forbidden zone. I am afraid that Mr. Sheaffer is guilty of blocking the nation's highways and causing an obstruction to traffic. There is an automatic fine of five pounds for this offence.'

Sheaffer reached into his wallet and handed the sergeant five pounds, thanking him, as he did so, for the lightness of the charge and making a few brief remarks about human rights, justice, and the dignity of the law.

But just then, as he was about to take his third whist

game in succession, the door of the police station burst
open, the wind ripped a WANTED notice from the wall, and
the highest agent of Her Majesty's Secret Service came
into the room amidst a flurry of dead and sodden leaves.
Cartwright had found his man.

24

AND yet, even at that moment, when the toppling fortunes of Cartwright seemed to have righted themselves once more, the great man felt, within the pit of his being, grave doubts that the mysterious toothpaste heir who studied sex and killed off spies in bars with strange names could possibly be chained within the confines of this flimsy edifice. Numbing fatigue and the heaviness of his worn-out legs were slowing him up; he knew what he had come for, and why, but how on earth he was going to explain it to other people he just didn't know. Beatrice followed him into the station looking none too sure of herself; Lucy, walking beside her, had never been sure of herself; and Cartwright, who had from an early age always been sure of himself, had never really been terribly sure about other people. Difficult though he knew it would be, he tried to open his onslaught in the station with courtesy and restraint.

'Good evening,' he said.

'Good evening,' said the sergeant, eyeing with displeasure the sodden leaves that had come into the station along with Cartwright and friends.

'Beatrice!' exclaimed Sheaffer, looking up from his cards. 'Good Lord, what are you doing here?'

Beatrice tried to smile, failed, tried again, failed again, and wondered if indeed Sheaffer was as unworthy as unworthy Raymond.

'Does he mean you, Amanda?' asked Cartwright.

. . . Amanda . . . lies . . . Holy Moses . . .

'What can I do for you?' the sergeant asked.

'A question of condoms,' said Cartwright profoundly.

There was a pregnant silence. Sheaffer wondered what Beatrice was doing there, wondered what he was doing there himself, and even caught himself wondering what condoms were.

'I suppose,' said Cartwright patronisingly, 'that you are wondering what condoms are?'

'To tell you the truth,' said the good-natured sergeant, who was badly read out of choice, 'I've never heard of them before in my life.'

. . . Condoms . . . Salt and pepper . . . various spices . . . stir and add condoms . . .

'They are contraceptive sheaths,' said Cartwright, in the omniscient voice of a quiz-programme chairman, 'which are employed in sexual intimacy to prevent venereal disease and the procreation of offspring.'

'Oh yes,' said the sergeant, smiling in benign ignorance.

'He means French Letters,' said one policeman, sniggering as if he had just heard or told a diabolically wicked joke. 'Send him down to the chemist's—if they're still open, that is.'

'This is no light matter,' said Cartwright ominously. 'The Prime Minister is deeply concerned.'

There was an uncomfortable silence.

'This man,' Cartwright began, pointing in the direction of Sheaffer's abdomen, 'is called Sheaffer. Am I not correct in that?'

Beatrice nodded.

'Yes,' said the sergeant, 'he is.'

'He is a spy,' said Cartwright.

Sheaffer burst into spasms of laughter, breaking the dulled silence in a strange and eerie fashion.

'He is a man of spirit,' said the sergeant. 'What has he done?'

'This is *no* joke,' said Cartwright, who had not laughed for some days. 'I should explain to you who I am. My name is Cartwright.'

'Cartwright!' repeated one policeman, taken aback.

Sheaffer continued to bubble with laughter.

'Not *the* Cartwright?' said another policeman.

'You mean you're . . . ?' said the sergeant, in astonishment.

'Yes, I'm Cartwright,' said Cartwright. 'You may have heard of my exploits in the Paris slums and the Liberian jungles. You appreciate now, I hope, the gravity of the situation?'

'Grave indeed,' said the sergeant.

Sheaffer stopped laughing; his face dropped, and he looked unmistakably distressed. So Beatrice *was* involved; and *that* was what occupational therapy was all about; how he wished he had looked it up in the dictionary instead of relying on intuition.

'A chest was brought here,' said Cartwright. 'May I see it?'

'It's on the floor,' said the sergeant, 'beneath the dart board.'

Cartwright strode across to the tea chest. And then the door of the station suddenly burst open again, and Father Scraw rushed up to the desk, past Cartwright, past Beatrice, past Lucy, and past everything that was going on.

'Where's Sheaffer?' he demanded of the sergeant, his eyes bulging, his sharp nose a rich crimson.

'Here,' said Sheaffer just as Father Scraw recognised him.

'Good Lord—the bishop,' blurted Cartwright, stopping dead above the chest of books.

Beatrice whispered something into Cartwright's left ear.

'Beatrice,' exclaimed Father Scraw. 'You here too?'

'Everyone seems to be here,' said the muddled sergeant.

'Arrest that man, Sergeant,' said Cartwright, pointing to Father Scraw. 'I have reason to believe he is implicated in this awful deed.'

'Dear God,' said Father Scraw, 'I help a man with one hand and he smiteth me with the other. Acts fourteen, verse twenty-seven.'

'Have a seat, Father,' said the sergeant, crossing to the tea chest. 'Sir,' he barked pointedly at Cartwright, 'I'm afraid I cannot go around arresting men of God without reason.'

'You can't arrest me anyway,' said Father Scraw, calming down. 'In fact, I could kill you all this very instant and you couldn't do a thing about it. Bishops can do no wrong.'

Everyone briefly thought about this. Beatrice wondered if perhaps Father Scraw *was* going to kill everyone. Lucy began to cry. Sheaffer went to the toilet to be sick.

'Stop that man,' roared Cartwright.

'He's just going to honk,' said one policeman.

'Do him good,' said Cartwright unsympathetically. He turned to the sergeant. 'You still refuse to arrest this man?' he demanded.

'Yes,' interrupted Father Scraw.

'Right,' said Cartwright. 'I want everyone to sit down.'

Chairs were fetched and everyone sat down and looked unhappy. Father Scraw mumbled something about outrage and said that although the Lord had said vengeance was his, he still liked his bishops to give him a hand dishing it out.

Keckings and gurglings and unhappy moans drifted from the direction of the toilet.

Standing beside the tea chest, Cartwright stared smoulderingly around the circle of chairs. Power, he thought, once more. To control destiny, that was what life was all about; make them cringe a bit or even throw up; he was born for this.

Sheaffer staggered back from the toilet looking like a man who has just been castrated with blunt scissors, and took a chair next to Beatrice. Father Scraw smiled kindly in his direction.

Cartwright took a deep breath. 'In this box,' he said, pointing down at the chest, 'are hidden secrets vital to the future of this nation.' He bent down and took a wet brown-paper package from the top of the chest. 'The secrets come from Russia,' he continued, 'as the two felons sitting in this room know full well.' No one in the room looked as if they knew anything full well.

'Dear God,' Father Scraw burst out. 'The man must have escaped from a loony-bin. This is sheer madness.'

Cartwright ignored the remark and ripped open the package. Twelve dozen condoms glistened in their airtight, double-wrapped pouches. Cartwright opened one of the pouches with a deftness that betrayed his long familiarity with the procedure.

Beatrice, muddled, forgot herself, and placed a soft hand on the top of Sheaffer's. 'Why did you do it?' she whispered.

'Silence, Amanda,' snapped Cartwright.

Sheaffer forced open an eye. 'I didn't,' he muttered.

Hope swelled in the heart of Beatrice. Not that she really felt for him; perhaps he was lying; lying like Raymond with the blue eyes and the little moustache she loved to tickle.

Cartwright, meanwhile, had stretched out one of the lubricated condoms and was trying to detect a trace of microfilm on it.

'Nothing there, is there?' said Father Scraw sneeringly. 'You great blithering idiot.'

'Shut his Holiness up,' Cartwright commanded the sergeant. He fished out another contraceptive. Still no success. And another. The crowd sat restless in their chairs. Cartwright tore savagely at the fourth pouch, cut his finger, and mumbled a few obscenities.

'I've had enough of this,' said Father Scraw in a very determined voice and fuming with rage. 'My steeple strewn across my beautiful house and lawn and this raving idiot uttering balderdash about espionage and accusing my best friend of it too. Sergeant, I demand that you release Mr. Sheaffer and myself.'

'I haven't even arrested you, Father,' said the sergeant. He turned to Cartwright. 'I agree with them, Mr. Cartwright,' he said, and rose from his chair.

'Let's have a game of cards,' said one policeman.

'And a drink,' suggested another. 'Thank God something exciting only happens here about once every seven years.'

'Hold it right there,' said Cartwright. They all stared at his eyes, and at the gun in his hand, shiny and black, that he had borrowed from Beatrice. 'No one will leave here until I say so.' Everyone froze.

'Shoot me, then,' said Father Scraw, advancing. 'Shoot a man of God.'

Cartwright put his finger on the trigger. Father Scraw fainted.

'See what you've done,' said the distressed sergeant, 'to good old Scraw, and on the very night he lost the steeple that was so dear to his heart.'

'Get a grip on yourself, man,' said one policeman.

Cartwright already felt he had a grip on himself. All this worry, all this way—the plane, the bus, and the spewing of ham sandwiches on the flora of Fife; all for what? For nothing; deceived at the last moment; no microfilm. Visions of long scrolls of income-tax returns wafted before his heavy eyes, but he held the gun steady.

'Where are they, Mr. Sheaffer?' he asked menacingly.

Beatrice tightened her grip on Sheaffer's hand. A policeman poured some whisky from Sheaffer's bottle down Father Scraw's throat, and he recovered consciousness immediately.

Cartwright held the gun in front of Sheaffer's nose. 'Tell me,' he demanded. 'Tell me where the real thing is, or I promise you—I'll shoot. You should know my reputation, Sheaffer.'

'Straight-shooting Cartwright,' said one policeman cynically.

'Terror of the force,' said another policeman, playing with a hand of cards and thinking about his dinner.

'Bloody idiot,' said Father Scraw, from his position on the floor.

Suddenly, amidst all the confusion, the station door burst open once more, and a tall, well-dressed man with a face that looked as if it ought to belong to someone famous marched into the now crowded station, accompanied by a small, frail woman.

'What have you done with my son?' he boomed. 'I am told he is here. There you are, lad. Good God, what have the buggers done to you?'

'Hold back,' ordered Cartwright, turning the gun on Ernest Sheaffer. 'Your son is a deadly criminal.'

'Oh, my poor baby,' squealed Ethel Sheaffer, rushing to her son and throwing her arms around his neck. 'My poor baby—what have they done to you?'

'Accused him of all manner of things falsely,' said Father Scraw. 'Good to see you again, Ethel.'

Cartwright pointed his gun directly at Sheaffer once more, turned, and said to Ernest, 'My name is Cartwright, sir. Your son stole contraceptives—contraceptives with government secrets printed on them. Your son is a spy.'

'Dear me, never,' whined Ethel Sheaffer. 'My poor baby wouldn't know what a contraceptive looked like.'

'I certainly wouldn't, Mummy,' said Sheaffer.

Beatrice released her grip on his hand and began stroking it tenderly. 'I think he's innocent,' she said, almost loudly, and wondered how she had ever come to that conclusion or summoned up the courage to voice it.

Cartwright turned to Ernest Sheaffer, and a terrible sight met his eyes. In the split second he had looked away, Ernest had produced a massive weapon from within his coat and was now pointing the weapon at Cartwright's chest.

'Drop the gun,' said Ernest, earnestly.

Cartwright dropped the gun to the floor; it bounced twice and lay on its side against the book-filled tea chest.

'Shiver me truncheon,' said the sergeant, 'what next? We're bound to lose the crime-free shield now.'

'Damned disgrace,' said one policeman.

'Silence,' said Ernest Sheaffer. 'I'll have you know that no Sheaffer has been arrested since Abraham Sheaffer in 1642, and he was probably illegitimate. And that record is not going to change now. I have here in my hand,' he continued, indicating his weapon, 'an especially powerful device used for killing whales in southern waters. It shoots harpoons into them at something like two hundred miles an hour.'

Cartwright refused to shudder; just because it could kill a whale didn't mean it could kill a Cartwright.

'Don't be a fool,' he said. 'Let's talk this one out.'

'Start talking,' said Ernest, remembering a Western he had once seen.

'I'm starving,' said the policeman who had been thinking about his dinner.

'Go and bring some fish and chips, Horace,' said the sergeant to the same policeman, handing him Sheaffer's five-pound fine. 'Make it six fish suppers, one pie supper, two red puddings, a big haggis, and seventeen pickles. Who wants salt and pepper?'

'Me,' said Ernest Sheaffer. 'Plenty of salt. Now, Mr. Cartwright, start talking.'

'Last Thursday,' Cartwright began, 'your son took two packages from the London docks. These contained secrets vital to our country's future.'

'Incredible,' said Ernest scoffingly. 'Of course,' he said, looking towards his son, 'you know nothing about this, Sheaffer?'

'Oh, I took them,' said Sheaffer, 'I definitely did.'

Everyone looked aghast except Cartwright, who smiled in his most self-satisfied way.

'Ye gods,' said Ernest.

Ethel Sheaffer crossed herself. Beatrice stopped stroking Sheaffer's hand and looked at him in complete astonishment. Father Scraw raised his eyes to Heaven, and the sergeant hoped his fish supper would arrive before long.

'*You* took them,' said Ernest sternly to his son. 'You really took them?'

'I thought they were altar wine,' said Sheaffer, unperturbed. 'I always bring it up here when I come from London. When we discovered it was dirty books, we hid them in the attic.'

'There we are,' said Ernest. 'The perfect explanation.

Stick that in your pipe and smoke it, Cartwright.' He lowered his harpoon gun.

'Good old Sheaffer,' said a policeman.

'Spirited fellow,' said the sergeant, who had developed quite a soft spot for Sheaffer.

'Friend of the church and of God,' said Father Scraw chantingly.

'My own son,' said Ethel Sheaffer, stroking her son's cheek lovingly.

Beatrice felt wonderful but decided not to say anything.

'Fuck,' said Cartwright. 'If you didn't take the secrets, then where the hell are they?'

'*Here*,' said a voice from the door. The floor shook and began to rumble, and a man of almost seven feet, with arms as thick as telegraph poles and biceps like tree trunks, paced slowly and deliberately into the police station, past Ernest Sheaffer and the lowered harpoon gun, until he stood, towering in all his strength, amidst and above the assembled gathering. Heaving a deep sigh, he thrust a huge hairy hand into his jacket pocket and took from it a small metal canister, which he tossed to the incredulous Cartwright.

'Your secrets, George,' he said. Harold Wilcox had returned from the grave.

The Secret of
the Roaring Donkey

I

THE return of Harold Wilcox was universally approved
of and celebrated, both in Lindenlee and in the nation at
large. On the evening of his homecoming, not one hour after
he had given Cartwright the Russian secrets, the national
press, radio, and television descended upon the small Scottish town, clamouring for pictures, comments, and suitable
epithets for the next day's headlines, current-affairs pro-
grammes, and news broadcasts. Harold, it was generally
agreed, was his country's saviour, as he had been on many
previous occasions. Having supposedly died with a glass in
his hand, the papers said, he had, through the complicity of
a brilliant young sectologist and a great spiritual leader,
risen from the dead and gone on to play a leading part in
Britain's history. Naturally, however, no mention was made
in any of the press conferences that the reason Harold had
given his accomplices for his need to die was, in fact, that
he could not stand his wife any longer.

In great detail the story was told, wherever mass media
had a name worth living up to. There were pictures of
Harold himself, and of his reunion with Miriam. There
were pictures of him with a glass of Campbell's keg in one
hand and a Guinness in the other; and there were pictures
of him drinking a toast with Sheaffer and his father and
Cartwright, with Father Scraw and Ethel Sheaffer drinking
orange juice in the background for decency's sake. Then

there was a picture of Sheaffer working alone on sectological manuscripts and smoking furiously, and one of Father Scraw on top of the still-standing portion of the steeple, with a grave expression on his face and his new mitre on his head. Someone even managed to get Beatrice into a bathing costume, and the *Daily Globe* voted her 'Best-looking Young Spy of the Year'.

But the hero of the hour was undoubtedly old Tiger Wilcox himself. He even brushed up his grammar for the television interviews, and Miriam made him brush his hair and wear a tie. When he had first reappeared in the Roaring Donkey, she believed he was a ghost, but since ghosts were not known for their prodigious consumption of ale on toilet seats she soon realised that it was indeed her dear old Harold, returned by some miracle with all his bad habits intact. When she fully appreciated the extent of his duplicity, she resolved never to talk to him again; but since she had an exceeding fondness for the sound of her own voice and loved complaining to him about things, her silence survived only a few minutes, after which she threw her arms around him, told him he was the most wonderful man in the world, and promised never to pick her nose again, since she knew it irritated him.

Harold's interviews were, as it happened, a great success, even though he did slur his words from time to time when he had imbibed a little too much beforehand. In his deep, authoritative voice, which occasionally broke into spasms of ferocious laughter, Harold told of his final mission, given him by the Queen, to bring the vital Russian secrets back to Britain single-handed while everyone else believed them to be hidden in the contraceptives. Harold had carried them all the way in his coat pocket, that being the last place enemy agents would think of looking for them.

Naturally, the newspapers loved this story, since it made foreigners out to be rather naïve.

Harold's other mission, which for security purposes he was not allowed to tell the newspapers about, was to make a study of all the British agents along the way into whose hands the contraceptives, with false data printed on them, had fallen. Some of these spies, it turned out, had been dreadfully wicked and disloyal, and one of them had destroyed the false information on the condoms, believing it to be the real thing, and had replaced the original condoms with normal ones. Hence Cartwright's inability to find any messages printed on them.

The Prime Minister, Harold explained to his friends, knew nothing about the mission because he was considered to be an exceptionally silly man who couldn't keep his mouth shut and was only good at making speeches to the nation. Cartwright had obviously not been told because he knew many of the agents Harold was spying on and Her Majesty feared he might feel honour-bound to tell them they were being watched.

When Harold, flushed with the joys of life and fortified by a huge steak pie, had arrived back in London, he had dropped into Buckingham Palace to tell the Queen about all the double agents he had caught out. Then, while he was munching crumpets that the Queen had baked herself, just the way he liked them, news filtered through to the Palace that Cartwright had rushed off to Scotland in search of the worthless condoms. Thus Harold had to leave one crumpet half finished and did not even have time to kiss the Queen's hand before dashing off for the first plane north.

Events did not turn out too badly for Cartwright after all. As luck had it, his uncle Theodore controlled several London daily newspapers, and his performance in the entire episode was painted in rosy colours. It was suggested in editorials and gossip columns that he had, in fact, been in league with Tiger all the time and had only come to Lindenlee to retrieve the condoms for the British Espionage Museum, where they were to be put on public display for the winter. This pleased Cartwright very much, since he felt he had behaved in his usual determined fashion and had displayed a great deal of courage in the face of Ernest Sheaffer's harpoon gun. He was even interviewed on television, which, although he never admitted it, delighted him, for he had a much higher opinion of himself than anyone else he had ever met, and hoped that sentiment might be shared by others.

Yet despite his professed egotism, and partly because of it, Cartwright was in good company in Lindenlee, where there were many men and women of similar disposition. Following Harold's return, Cartwright and Lucy spent many hours drinking with Sheaffer, Beatrice, the sergeant, Harold and Mirian Wilcox, and, of course, Father Scraw, who would forgive anyone anything except unadulterated nastiness over a prolonged period of time. This leisurely company relaxed Cartwright, who had spent most of his previous life with dedicated people of one sort or another, and he began to realise for the first time since his youth that true happiness, although inaccessible, is more approachable when you do things on impulse instead of relying on a cool sense of logic. In his short time in Lindenlee he showed great interest in learning how to pour beer properly, which Harold Wilcox spent two hours teaching him, and he also discovered from Sheaffer the basic methodological processes involved in forming classical sectological thought.

So readily was Cartwright taken into the hearts of those in Lindenlee that he was exhorted to remain with Lucy for the party to be held at the end of the week in the Roaring Donkey to celebrate Tiger's triumphant return from foreign parts and his contribution to the realm. Cartwright, who had no gnawing urge to return immediately to his silent pink telephone, readily agreed. In the ensuing days, the festivities were prepared with meticulous care and great extravagance.

And what a party it was! Everyone in Lindenlee who had a sense of humour was there, and there was a notorious absence of lawyers, chartered accountants, justices of the peace, and anyone who was likely to put any kind of damper on things. Even Winifred Scraw was encouraged to come, and spent a quiet evening with Ethel Sheaffer beside the vodka bottle, which their husbands told them was full of Vichy water.

The food for the party was beyond compare. Besides exotic delicacies from both hemispheres, there were lots of homemade specialities: crumpets for Harold Wilcox with homemade strawberry jam, bowls full of toad-in-the-hole for Jack Bendex, and coconut buns aplenty prepared by Suzie Elliot, who for much of the evening was seen nuzzling up to a young professor of astro-botany. There were rum candies too, which Cartwright took particular delight in scoffing, when he wasn't dancing with Suzie Elliot's mother, who had made them, and with whom he had been spending much time during the previous few days. Rumours from reliable gossips had it that a certain primitive fondness had developed between them, which was really not such a bad thing, inasmuch as Mrs. Elliot's divorce was just coming through. Besides, Cartwright really needed a stable mature woman like Mrs. Elliot to love and care for and sleep with, and to learn from her how to treat women in the way they ought to be treated. Lucy Frome, far from feeling out of it, had built up a crush on Jack Bendex, who on the previous evening had given her a gold filling for free when one of her amalgam ones fell out; on such small things, she thought, is the heart of woman turned.

The heart of Beatrice was also much more prepared to be turned than it had in the indecisive moments of the previous weekend. As she stood at the party, looking at all the happy faces, as she danced the Hokey Cokey opposite Sheaffer, she realised how little Raymond and his suède jackets now meant to her. She was going to renounce espionage, concentrate on occupational therapy, and return to her cultivation of vegetables. If Sheaffer stayed in Lindenlee, well and good; if not, then that was the way it went; but of course he was going to stay.

'You *are* going to stay, Sheaffer?' she whispered, leaning across to him.

'Of course,' he replied.

Sheaffer was indeed going to stay. Professor Swish had spoken, as he had promised, to his father, and had told him that in days to come the words 'sects' and 'Sheaffer' would be inseparable in any decent dictionary. Moreover, because he had agreed to chair the monthly board meetings and to look at the *Financial Times* from time to time, his father had expressed no objection to his remaining in Lindenlee. In fact, old Ernest had been so excited about his son's assistant lectureship that he bought him a new aeroplane to celebrate and made him promise to fly out to Antarctica at Christmastime, bringing with him any friends he liked to. 'Our igloo will always be your igloo too, son,' he said, brimming with parental affection, love, and pride.

For Sheaffer, then, the party was a time of unqualified happiness. Surrounded by all his friends, the woman of his choice, the father who had taught him how to enjoy life, and the priest who had proved it was possible to do so, he glanced at the aesthetically fulfilling sight of the various bottles of red and blue, green and mauve, and just plain white or golden yellow, filled with strong and tasty fluids from all corners of the globe. Behind them, on a broad firm table, were many samples of all the beers brewed north and south of the Humber, from every English county and Scottish shire where the brewing of beer was at all possible. The trays of food stretched across the room; glasses, all of which were full or overflowing, glistened on the cluttered tables. The Fife Fiddlers had started up the 'Gay Gordons' with gusto; the air was hot but not too hot. He had a beautiful woman on his arm, but not so beautiful that he was likely to lose her; a feeling of warmth and light-headedness swept over him, an intoxication that would produce, for once, no hangover. It really was quite a night. His sexual problems had now slipped from the front of his mind; the sexule taken on Monday had not had much effect, but he had repeated the process over the next few days and had paid short visits to some old insatiables he had known in his randier days. And, as he now danced in these reassuring surroundings, he felt his former potency somewhere deep down within him. In a week, he knew, the days of old would have returned once more, though not to the same lascivious extent; the secret of happy hormones, he now knew, was a *controlled* horniness —the sentiments of the young lady concerned being the governing factor. Tactful restraint coupled with cautious optimism—that was what it was all about. Like life, he thought, as he reached across and took Beatrice's hand.

Throughout that truly wonderful evening, as the fiddlers played, the glasses were drained and filled again, and the luscious foods were consumed, spirits rose even more, until eventually, at midnight, when Harold Wilcox returned from polishing off six Guinness crumpets in the toilet, it was declared by one and all to be 'speech time'.

Harold Wilcox rose to his feet amidst deafening clamours of applause. That very day, he said, opening a bottle of Guinness and taking a hefty slug, he had received a telegram from the Queen. Henceforward he was to be known as Harold, First Baron Wilcox, and he was to go to Buckingham Palace on the following Tuesday to be confirmed in this honour and to have some more crumpets, which the Queen would again prepare herself in the royal kitchens. Many hands tried to pat Harold on the back, but unfortunately his back was too high up for that; he simply smiled benignly down on his admirers.

Furthermore, he added, he had been offered a pension of ten thousand pounds a year for life, which, after a couple of seconds' serious consideration, he had decided to accept. However, he would continue running the Roaring Donkey until at last he died a proper death. He went on to praise his dear wife, who had gone through so much hardship in the unconscious service of her country, and Mrs. Wilcox smiled lovingly, moved to pick her nose, remembered her promise, and swallowed half a glass of brown ale in one gulp instead.

Harold having sat down, Father Scraw was vigorously encouraged to say a few words. This he was most loath to do, because he had drunk so much he was not in a fit state even to speak to himself. However, being as ever willing to please, he was assisted from his chair with glass in hand and his beer-stained mitre topping his head, and was eventually propped up against a strong table, where he began to speak. Life, said Father Scraw, with snail-like precision and slowness, was like Christianity, in that it was an osmotic process.

There was a long pause after this while everyone who did not know what osmotic meant had it explained to them by someone who did. After that the applause was deafening, and it was widely agreed that Father Scraw had probably been writing theological manuals under pseudonyms for years. Despite the loud cries of 'more, more', Father Scraw was incapable of saying anything else, and with slurred words he concluded by saying simply that since he was now a bishop, he would be very glad to use his extra influence to put in a good word with 'Him up there' for any of his friends present. And with that remark he indicated the conventionally accepted position of Heaven with an upturned finger, fell supine upon the table, and was helped back to his seat by Sheaffer.

The pressure of speaking now fell upon Cartwright, who from his original dearth of popularity in the town had risen to such an extent in people's estimation that there were several chants of 'Cartwright, Cartwright!' before he finally could be persuaded to get up.

Cartwright was very nervous when he began to speak. Except for his brief appearance on television, he had never spoken in public before, and for the first time in his life he sensed that he was surrounded by people who felt a certain degree of affection for him. Embarrassed as he was by this mysterious environment, Cartwright's face was bright red, and, as he spoke, he stood in a slightly crouched and uncomfortable stance.

First he said how deeply moved he was that everyone had treated him so kindly. 'Good old George!' someone shouted; it was the first time anyone had ever said that about Cartwright, and he was visibly touched. After taking a big sip of his drink, he told everyone that he was going to resign his job in the Secret Service and go back to being a private detective in London. Administrative duties, he said, were not for him; he was going back to following people and tracking them down; that, he said, was what would make him happy. And the only other thing that had ever made him happy, except for something which decency prevented mention of, was being in Lindenlee, where he had met some wonderful people. And with that comment he leered lecherously at Susan Elliot's mother, who leered lecherously back, and everyone thought what a good match they were—including Lucy Frome, who was curled up in Jack Bendex's lap.

Then it was Beatrice's turn to speak. She was shaking like a feather in a wind, and her diminutive form amidst all these big people made her look rather like the fairy on the top of a huge Christmas tree. She started to say something, paused, and stopped. Then she smiled; it was such a little smile that if anyone else had smiled it you might not even have thought it a smile at all; then it grew somewhat, and then slowly she drew her lips together again; then she sat down; and everyone in the room felt that smile was for them. And one person in particular was sure it was for him.

He was the next to speak, and the last. Fond of making speeches, he had been looking forward to this moment all night, and so when everyone made it clear that they wanted him to speak, Sheaffer picked up his glass and walked to the front of the room.

'Good evening,' he began. This was, of course, an entirely unnecessary remark, but feeling, as he did, that his speeches were better than anyone else's, he wanted to make it sound quite formal. 'This party,' he went on, 'is for the First Baron Wilcox.' Everyone knew this very well, but being used to Sheaffer's speeches, and, in a strange sense, being very partial to them, they found the remark almost brilliant.

'Baron Wilcox and Lady Miriam are wonderful people.'

'Hear, hear,' roared the guests.

'Moreover,' said Sheaffer, pausing deliberately for a silence that he expected and got, 'Baron Wilcox has proved that it is not only possible to drink and work at the same time. He has proved it is possible to drink too much and work better.'

Since almost everyone present sympathised with this sentiment entirely, the applause lasted for several minutes.

'But there is *one* thing,' said Sheaffer, raising his voice, 'which no one has bothered to ask during this whole crisis involving the lasting security of our country. Has anyone any idea what it is?'

Sheaffer looked round at the blank fuddled faces.

'A simple point,' he continued, 'but a very important one, and that is: What was the best British agent this century has produced doing working in a small Scottish town that only a handful of people have ever heard of? Why was he sent here, of all places—the mighty Tiger, who has instilled terror in the hearts of thousands? Why on earth should he be stationed in Lindenlee?'

A hundred eyes stared and wondered and waited.

'The reason is this,' Sheaffer said. 'Harold Wilcox came to Lindenlee because I asked that he come.'

An intense silence pervaded the room. A glass chinked, and then there was silence once more.

'Let me show you something,' said Sheaffer. He pulled a vacant chair across the floor and stood on it. Protecting his hand with a handkerchief, he took a light bulb from its socket and pressed a small button inside. The rear wall of the Roaring Donkey slid smoothly and gently aside to the soft whirr of a well-oiled engine.

'Suffering synagogues,' said Father Scraw, gasping in amazement; and they all gasped, everyone in the room. Then

they sat motionless, transfixed by the scene before them—
all but Harold Wilcox, who sat sleeping in his chair. In the
spot where the rear wall had stood a vast vault had opened
up, and within the vault were hundreds of shelves of steel.
On the shelves lay ingots, gold ingots, piled neatly and sym-
metrically, row upon row upon row. Sheaffer walked into
the vault, picked up an ingot, and threw it with a dull thud
on to the floor of the Roaring Donkey.

'The gold reserves of our country,' he said calmly. 'The
gold reserves, intact, secured in vaults here and below the
Roaring Donkey, and in safes so strong that no man or
mechanical device can ever lay hands on them. What is
more,' he added, 'I am their keeper.'

The company sat numbed with awe, staring at Sheaffer,
then at the gold, then at Sheaffer once more.

'Seven years ago,' he went on, 'the security of the reserves
was threatened. The Bank of England decided they should
be hidden in secret vaults somewhere in the country where
no master criminals would think to look for them. And so
I was summoned to London to meet the governor. Why
was *I* summoned? Well, you see, there is a part of my life
that none of you know anything about, because I rarely think
about it and *never* speak about it. When I was young and
in school, I was never permitted to study sects, and so I grew
bored. And all day long I dabbled with locks, until, in time,
I came up with an invention that locksmiths had sought
for years—the four-piece reversible psychotic lock, totally
amorphous, and powered by an inverted prismial configura-
tion of the sun's rays. In my laboratory in Provence I per-
fected the lock, but this was the first time it had ever been
tried out for real—and I was concerned, very concerned—
for the sun's rays do not shine as often in this part of the
country as my locks would wish. So I asked the governor of

the bank to find me the best spy in Britain to help me watch over the safety of the gold in its initial stages. You see, I knew Harold Wilcox was a spy, but when he said he had to disappear, I asked no questions. I knew nothing about his mission—one trusts one's friends. Incidentally, you will note that none of you have ever seen me on a Sunday afternoon or evening.' Sheaffer paused again and glanced around. Father Scraw, Jack, Professor Swish, Suzie Elliot, and her mother were all nodding their heads slowly in agreement.

'And the reason for that,' said Sheaffer, 'is that during that time I came here, by my secret entrance, to check all my beautiful locks. Tomorrow the gold will be taken elsewhere. Because of the recent rumpus, it is no longer safe in Lindenlee and it will pass into the hands of another. But I thought that before you left you should all know how very important our little town once was.'

'Diabolical deck chairs!' said Ernest Sheaffer. 'Sons never tell their fathers anything nowadays.'

'My *father* never told *me* anything,' said Cartwright, choking with raucous laughter. 'I had to learn it all myself—by hand.'

'And now,' said Sheaffer from the centre of the floor, 'let me just close and propose a toast, by employing the immortal words of Shakespeare: "To every thing there is a season, and a time to every purpose under the heaven." The purpose of this time and season is revelry. Let us have a toast.'

The guests quickly replenished their glasses from suitably handy bottles.

'To Miriam Wilcox and the resurrected Tiger.'

The clash of glasses that followed echoed across the cluttered tables of the Roaring Donkey. All eyes turned to the reunited couple—Mrs. Wilcox with her shining face and watering eyes, and Harold, his massive form ensconced in an armchair with an empty glass of Campbell's special keg in his hand and an expression on his face that demonstrated beyond any doubt that he was in a state of suspended inebriation. His eyes were fixed and glassy, his lips thick, sealed, and motionless, like those of a waxwork model; his massive form was static; nothing moved.

'*Harold!*' Miriam shouted boisterously. 'Harold, wake up, dear.'

But Harold Wilcox did not move, and a low murmur spread across the room. The murmur broke into concern, the concern into panic, and everyone felt deep within him the same awful feeling.

'Lord, no,' said Father Scraw. 'Not again!'

'God,' gasped Beatrice.

'Heavens above!' moaned Ernest Sheaffer.

'Jesus Christ!' breathed Suzie Elliot, clasping the professor of astro-botany's hand more firmly on her breast.

Cartwright said, 'Fuck.'

Mrs. Wilcox was tugging at Harold's arm and shouting at him at the top of her voice. The brimful glasses hung in the air; drink poured on the floor; no one moved except Sheaffer. Smiling broadly, he walked across the floor, knelt down, whispered something into the left ear of Harold Wilcox, and took the empty glass from his hand.

A waxen smile slowly spread across the thick lips, the eyes flickered gently, and the mouth of the First Baron Wilcox opened wide once more.

'One for the road, lad,' he said.